UNDUE INFLUENCE

JENNY HOLIDAY

Undue Influence

Copyright © 2018 by Jenny Holiday

Edited by Sarah Lyons. Copyedited by Heather Martin. Cover design by Zack Taylor. Cover photo by olly19, Deposit Photos.

First edition, September 2018

ISBN: 978-1-7753768-1-1 (e-book)

ISBN: 978-1-7753768-2-8 (paperback)

She had been forced into prudence in her youth, she learned romance as she grew older: the natural sequel of an unnatural beginning.

—Jane Austen, *Persuasion*

CHAPTER ONE

"'It is a truth universally acknowledged, that—'"

"Oh, fuck off."

Playing dumb, Adam manufactured a confused look and aimed it at his sister. "Pardon me?" No matter that Betsy was pushing thirty, Adam still enjoyed bugging his big sister.

She rolled her eyes and waved her hands vigorously in the air in an attempt to dry her freshly painted fingernails. "You *know* that's not what I meant when I asked you to read to us."

Adam's mother heaved a put-upon sigh. Wilhelmina Elliot, of Kellynch Vineyards in Bishop's Glen, New York, was a woman who, unless there was a gun to her head, never read anything but *Page Six*. Or, in a pinch, the crime report in the *Bishop's Glen Bulletin*.

Unlike her daughter, though, the Elliot matriarch would never resort to vulgar language to register her disapproval. She merely murmured, "Language," at Betsy, then pointed a shiny purple talon—her nails were wet, too—at a stack of newspapers and magazines on the floor next to the sofa.

"You'd both like this book if you gave it a chance, I think,"

Adam said even as he exchanged it for the *Post*. "There's lots of conniving in it."

"Lots of what?" Betsy blew on her fingers.

Adam tried not to roll his eyes as he shook *Page Six Magazine* out of the *Post*. Something caught in his chest to think that this might be the last time they did this. Was he going to...miss this?

No. That was crazy. He was going to miss Kellynch something fierce—losing the vineyard was going to be like losing a limb—but this weird, nineteenth-century-esque ritual in which his relatives summoned him to read to them while their nails dried was a prime example of why he'd moved out of the house four years ago. He loved his mom and sister, and he believed they loved him, in their way. Getting to a place where that was true had not been easy. Theirs was a hard-won affection, and easier to maintain when he could love them from afar, from his cozy, *solitary* motorhome among the vines at the far end of the property.

But still. Once more for posterity. He cleared his throat. "Paris Hilton's dog died, and she's planning a funeral with—"

"This is old news." Betsy waved her hands again but this time in a dismissive rather than a nail-drying gesture. The fact that he could tell the difference was probably pretty pathetic.

"Well, I'm not sure print is the most efficient format for the timely delivery of gossip." He got out his phone. "Is the Wi-Fi still on?" The electricity was, so maybe it would be. But, no. And he'd be damned if he used any of his data to read the gossip pages to his mom and sister. Like them, he was broke. Unlike them, he was not in denial about it. Tomorrow morning, he was moving his RV from the estate to his brother's yard in town, and nothing about his modest existence would change—except of course for the fact that his heart, such as it was, would remain behind, tangled up in the vines at Kellynch.

But he was resigned. He had plenty of experience walking around with a broken heart. Freddy had made sure of that.

No, *Rusty* had made sure of that.

No, that wasn't fair. Adam had no one to blame but himself for the state of his heart.

"What I really want to know is what's going on in the *Hamptons*." Betsy slumped theatrically against the back of the sofa but kept her arms in the air so as not to mar her manicure. She looked like a zombie taking a rest.

"You'll find out firsthand soon enough," Adam said.

"I can't *stand* that we couldn't leave today. Tonight's the Art Hamptons opening party, you know, and Charlie has tickets."

He did know. She'd been talking of nothing else since it was decided that she and their mother would take a family friend up on an invitation to join him in the Hamptons for a few weeks. Adam feared that "take Charlie up on his invitation for a few weeks" was actually a euphemism for them having invited themselves for an indefinite stay, but honestly, he was too exhausted to care. For the most part, he'd made his peace with carrying out his duty to his family, but clearing out the house had been both physically demanding and heartbreaking, and he needed a breather from babysitting them.

Charlie had been a professional friend of Dad's through the New York Wine & Grape Foundation. He'd been in touch after Dad's death and had helped set them up with the ultimately unsuccessful winemaker who'd taken over—not that Adam blamed either the winemaker or Charlie. You couldn't do something with nothing, and at the rate his family spent money after Dad's death, what they'd had to work with was basically "nothing."

He sort of felt like Charlie had done enough for their family, but Adam was so tired. His leg required a lot of rest at the best of times, given his dogged commitment to walking everywhere. And this was not the best of times. So he was just going to let Charlie have his mom and sister for a while.

Betsy sighed. "If only we could have left *today*."

"I don't know what to tell you," Adam said. "Mom has to be here for the auction tomorrow." He might do everything around here, but on paper the vineyard belonged to Wilhelmina—for one more day, anyway.

"Adam, you need your hair cut." His mother was pretending she hadn't heard anything. Just like she was pretending their home wasn't going into foreclosure. Pretending she and Betsy hadn't run the family business in to the ground. "Your features are too delicate for long hair."

"It's not *long*." It wasn't the short-sided, fascist cut she preferred on him, and yes, maybe he was a bit overdue for a trim, but no reasonable person would call it long. But then, when had his mother ever been reasonable?

"The limp is enough, dear. You don't need another unusual feature to draw people's attention."

Isn't drawing people's attention one of your favorite pastimes?

He kept his mouth shut, though. There was no point. He'd long since learned that he could either have a family or not have one, and if he wanted one, it came at a cost.

"Not to mention the gay thing," his sister added.

Yes. The gay *thing*. Adam sighed. A shaggy-haired, gay guy with a limp: what a scandal. Thankfully, the *gay thing* really *wasn't* a thing anymore. To his mother's credit, after an initial freak-out, she'd gotten over his coming-out at age seventeen pretty quickly. It generally didn't appear on her laundry list of his shortcomings—or at least very high on that list.

"Today's *Bulletin* is here, isn't it?" his mother asked, apparently having lost interest in criticizing his appearance. "You didn't have them stop the subscription until tomorrow, right?"

"Yep." Adam opened the local paper to the crime blotter. "Drunk and disorderly, Stone Road."

"That's Glen Lake Estates." Betsy, naming another of the local vineyards, perked up.

"Officers were called to investigate a disturbance created by two men who became incensed when told a tour package they purchased did not come with unlimited refills." Adam chuckled. "One of the individuals, upon talking to an officer, elected to upgrade to the unlimited option. The other grew increasingly belligerent and was arrested for drunk and disorderly conduct."

His mother sniffed. "I'm not sure what they expect with those..." She wrinkled her nose. "Tours." Bringing people in on buses like that. *Honestly.* I wouldn't want a sip, much less an unlimited amount of any of Glen Lake's so-called Riesling."

Adam refrained from pointing out that Glen Lake, unlike Kellynch, was thriving. Those busloads of tourists his mother found so beneath her kept the place afloat. The time for those arguments was done, though. You couldn't undo foreclosure. She'd never listened anyway, when Adam had tried to explain that from a simple accounting perspective, expenses could not exceed income indefinitely. Even he, who had never been a scholar or known much about the winemaking side of things, could understand that much.

He went back to the newspaper. "Domestic disturbance. Forty-eight-hundred block of Rook Street in Uppercross."

Betsy narrowed her eyes and pursed her lips. She was trying to figure out who it might be. "A twenty-five-year-old male summoned police to report that his estranged girlfriend threw a Bible at him."

"Oh! That's Henry McGuire!" Betsy exclaimed.

"It certainly is." Wilhelmina sniffed some more. There was nothing his mother enjoyed more than subtly displaying her disapproval and therefore her superiority. "Charlotte Haywick threw a Bible at Henry McGuire? She's in seminary—can you imagine? Acting like that when you're supposed to be...godly?"

"It's not really seminary," Betsy said. "It's some kind of weird hippie thing."

"I think it's just Unitarianism," Adam said. It wasn't like Charlotte was in the Hollywood cult Betsy had flirted with enough a few years ago that Adam had basically had to kidnap and deprogram her. But he took her point. Charlotte Haywick and Henry McGuire had a longstanding on-again, off-again relationship—they had since high school. Everyone always assumed they would end up together, but there certainly had been a lot of drama along the way. It kept the entire town riveted.

The old mantel clock chimed nine o'clock. Adam put down the newspaper. "Sorry, but I need to get this room done."

The library was the last room left to pack up. His mom and sister, given their indifference to books, had left it to the end —or, rather, left it to Adam, as they did pretty much every unpleasant task. It was also the only room in the house that had any furniture left in it, hence their having commandeered it for foreclosure-eve manicures. Because God forbid they be forced to vacate the home and vineyard that had been in their family for three generations without their nails done. They already thought it a terrible sacrifice that they'd had to give up their weekly mani-pedi salon appointments. *It's not extravagance,* his sister had protested. *It's just the bare minimum of what's considered socially acceptable.*

A flare of anger ignited in Adam's chest. He was pissed at his mother for letting their family's legacy crash and burn. She took no responsibility for anything, and she never would—and she had taught her daughter the same. His younger brother, Mark, wasn't much better, but at least he had his own house, so he wasn't so much Adam's problem.

When Adam's father was alive, he'd managed to keep the family's profligacy in check, but as hard as Adam had tried, he hadn't been able to replicate the feat and had been forced to watch Kellynch slowly bleed out over the last several years.

But it was useless to be angry with them. Wilhelmina and Betsy were professional martyrs. He could either accept that and have a family, or fight against it and be cast out.

And Adam was nothing if not practical.

And while he had done his best to try to keep things going at Kellynch after his dad died, all his interventions had accomplished was to prolong the inevitable. Now he just wanted to be done. And this was the last task: sorting through the books.

"Are your nails dry?" he asked his mom and sister. "Why don't you head out to your hotel, and I'll finish up here?"

"I thought it would be best if you did this room," his mother said. He didn't bother pointing out that he'd done *every* room.

"Will you see us off in the morning?" his sister asked.

"I can't. I have to work." *Some of us earn our living.*

"Oh, Rusty will give you the morning off," his mother said. Adam didn't want the morning off, was the thing. "He

can't. We have a transmission that's giving us major problems, and the mayor needs a flat replaced before ten o'clock
because he has to drive to Seneca Falls for a meeting."

"Well." His mother stood and brushed her hands together
as she looked around the half-packed room. "I guess that's it,
then."

"I guess it is."

"Really, it's for the best," his sister said. "I never liked—"

"Text me when you arrive safely." Adam pitched his voice
to drown her out because, God help him, he only had so much
patience. If his sister started up with one of her sour-grapes—
no pun intended—rants about how boring and sleepy Kellynch
and Bishop's Glen were, he could no longer be responsible for
his actions.

Adam loved this town. His grandmother had been one of
its most prominent residents back in the day, and he couldn't
imagine living anywhere else. Yes, it was kind of dull and was
slightly down-at-heels aside from the slice of it right along the
lake where the wealthy residents and summer people lived,
but it also had vines and forests and the big blue lake. It was
home. And given that he no longer had Kellynch, at least he
still had Bishop's Glen.

Finally, following a flurry of air kisses and hands-off hugs
—got to protect those nails—he was alone.

He opened a bottle of pinot noir, one of the last ones from
the harvest five years ago, the last year his father had overseen
things. He shouldn't have let it age this long, but he'd been
saving the last few bottles for a special occasion, and saying
goodbye to Kellynch was certainly "special."

There were no wineglasses left. His dad had kept a tray of
fine crystal ones in the library, which had been his retreat, but
they'd been sold off months ago. So he drank straight from

the bottle, deeply, letting the herby, berry-inflected vintage slide down his throat. Drinking from the bottle suited him anyway. If there hadn't been a vineyard in the family, Adam would have been a beer drinker, and probably a mass-produced macro-brew drinker at that. He'd never been as refined as his mother wanted. Or as ambitious as his best friend Rusty wanted. He was a guy who fixed cars by day and puttered around the vineyard by night, doing what he could to keep things in repair. Trying in vain to make his mother see that they needed to do things differently or they'd lose everything.

The wine was good. Pinot was a finicky grape for this cool-climate region, but the weather had cooperated that year, and his dad really had had the touch. His grandma had been competent as a winemaker, one of the region's pioneers in experimenting with cold-weather varietals, but his dad had been *great*. He'd been trying to make Kellynch into a real player in the region, and he'd been starting to see some success—some local awards and a few new, big wholesale clients. They'd even started talking about spiffing the place up so they could open themselves up to the public for tours and tastings.

But then he up and died.

If only he had allowed Adam to help him, like Adam's grandma had, Adam might have known enough to save things once his dad was gone. Grandma had been content to let ten-year-old Adam trail around behind her as she did the leaf thinning, making way for the sunshine to hit the clumps of fruit, but he'd been too young to really absorb anything. His dad, by contrast, had been focused on Betsy taking over as winemaker. Adam was never sure if it was because she was the oldest or because she was the not-gay one. The one without the limp.

Either way, he certainly had picked wrong. Betsy had never been interested in the actual work that went on at Kellynch, merely in the spoils of that work.

By contrast, whenever Adam volunteered his services, he'd been rebuffed. The winter pruning was too delicate a job, his dad would insist. He didn't know *how* he knew what temperature to ferment the Riesling at, he just knew. It wasn't teachable. You had to have a knack.

Eventually, Adam had gotten the message and stopped offering.

He allowed himself a few more swigs of wine before replacing the cork. He wanted to keep drinking, to just leave his head tilted back and chug, but there was work to be done. He gathered old newspapers and magazines and made a pile for recycling. Then he turned his attention to the books. A fair number of them, like the Austen he'd jokingly tried to read earlier, were his. He'd never bothered moving them to the RV, figuring there was plenty of room in the house, but now he would. The winemaking tomes that had been his grandmother's, and then his father's, he was less sure about. It felt like a sin to throw them away. The industry in the region was young, at least on a global scale. His grandmother had been the first winemaker at Kellynch, and he remembered her bringing these books back from trips to France, pouring over them in this very room.

Yet what good would it do to hold on to them? As of tomorrow, Kellynch Estates Winery would no longer belong to the Elliots. It remained to be seen whether the new owners would even bother trying to restore it to viability as a vineyard.

He sighed and flipped open the front cover of the book he'd been torturing his sister with. Rusty had given it to him eight years ago, just after he'd talked Adam into making the biggest mistake of his life.

He had inscribed the inside.

Austen had it wrong. There's no such thing as too much pride—or too much prejudice. xoxo, Lady RM.

CHAPTER TWO

Freddy glanced at his buzzing phone, which he'd left visible next to his workstation, as he chopped fennel.

`We got it.`

He poured himself a whiskey, picked up the phone, and took both items out the back door into the alley behind the restaurant.

Another text from his sister arrived before he could type a reply to the first one.

`Thank you so much for helping with this.`

He'd been glad to do it. Just because he personally loathed that shithole of a town didn't mean he wasn't happy to help his sister.

`Freddy: This was a foreclosure, right?`

He'd lost track of the properties his sister and her husband had considered during their search—part of his aversion to all things Bishop's Glen, probably.

Sophie: Yep. So we got it for a steal.

It was sad, really. The Finger Lakes region was home to some pretty, thriving towns. Bishop's Glen, though, was smack dab in the middle—in what his friend and business partner Ben called "the armpit of the Finger Lakes." Too far west for people from upstate and New York City, and too far east for people from Rochester and Buffalo, it was the kind of town where the surrounding wineries used wine slushies to attract Groupon-toting tourists.

Wine. Slushies.

He shuddered.

According to his sister, who was moving back to the region from Rochester, where she had settled with her husband, there had been a lot of foreclosures in the area. He'd told her to just buy what she wanted, no need to get involved with a foreclosure.

Sophie: I promise we'll pay you back.

Freddy: Soph, stop it. I have more money than I know what to do with. I'm happy to help.

Sophie: Still. Once Geordie gets his business off the ground, we are paying you back. I'm going to set up a payment plan.

Sophie's husband had, thanks to a severe knee injury, been forced into medical retirement from the navy. He had a mind to open a business taking tourists on lake cruises, which would probably be successful. His brother-in-law was smart and a hard worker, and all those wine-slushie-guzzling tourists needed something to do when they sobered up, didn't they?

Freddy: Whatever. The idea of you buying a place in Bishop's Glen is payment enough. You will have gone from cleaning those places to owning one. It's very satisfying.

It was true. He and his sister had grown up helping their single mother clean hotel rooms in that goddamn town, and now Sophie was going to own a piece of it. It was a nice bit of poetic justice.

Freddy: In fact, I hope you sit on your porch drinking wine and looking down your nose at those bitches who used to give you so much grief.

Sophie: Ha! I'm with you in spirit, but it's going to be hard to action that because the house isn't visible from the road. We actually bought an entire vineyard!

Freddy: Even better. Good for you.

Fuck all those assholes who thought he and Sophie would never amount to anything. Fuck. Them. Very. Much.

Sophie: It's not really functional right now
—there hasn't been a harvest in several
years, and the vines are all out of control,
but we didn't buy it for the vines. It has
good water access and lots of outbuildings
where Geordie can work on the boats. And
Freddy—it's BEAUTIFUL. I love it.

Freddy took a swig of his whiskey and smiled. His sister
wasn't vengeful like he was. She probably really did love the
place. He was glad about that, but he was also tickled by the
notion of one of the peasants taking over the means of
production.

Sophie: Maybe someday we can get it going
again as a working vineyard, but for now
we're just going to get settled and get the
boating business going.

Honestly, Freddy would rather she let the grapes rot in
place while she swanned around all day eating bonbons, but
that wasn't her.

Sophie: Will you come visit? Pretty please?

She knew about his aversion to Bishop's Glen, if not the
chief reason behind it. He had half a mind to make an appearance just to freak everyone the fuck out. *Yes, motherfuckers, I'm
back.* They'd all thought he was such a bad seed back in the
day. A little drinking, some poorly done tattoos. Some
sleeping around—including one time he got caught getting his
dick sucked in the town square by the son of a prominent

16

summer family. It didn't help that he and Sophie had different fathers, neither of whom had stuck around long enough to meet their kids. His had been a migrant worker—they came in the late summer to pick the grapes—who'd left before his mom even knew she was pregnant.

These things had combined to brand Freddy the bad boy of Bishop's Glen. All he'd wanted to do was keep his head down and work, both to help out his mom and, ultimately, as a means of propelling himself as far out of that shithole as humanly possible as soon as he could get enough money together.

But they wouldn't let him.

What would Adam have said? *Every story needs an antagonist.* At the time, Freddy had laughed at that interpretation. Thought that if he was the villain of Bishop's Glen, the Beast, then Adam was his Beauty. The only person pure of heart enough to see past the facade.

But no. He'd been wrong. He'd been so very wrong.

His phone pinged again.

Sophie: I know you have a hate-on for this place, but just THINK about coming, okay? Mom was talking about visiting later in the summer—you could fly into Rochester and drive her.

He'd be there sooner than she realized. Normally, his pride would not permit him to visit, even for his sister's sake. He'd left after that horrible night and vowed to never look back. And he hadn't. He'd learned from his mistake, hardened his heart, and made something of himself in spite of all those assholes. Maybe because of them.

Fuck. He could still see Adam's face crumpling. And Freddy had felt *bad* for him, even though Adam had been the one doing the dumping. His guts churned. Even after all these years, the memory had the power to trigger a visceral reaction. He *hated* that.

He needed to get a hold of himself. Look at him: he was rich and successful. He could handle a couple weeks in Bishop's Fucking Glen.

Freddy: You're gonna get your wish sooner rather than later, sis. Ben will be on his way to town soon, and fuck me, but I'm going to have to come with him.

Sophie: Oh, I'm a terrible person! I should have asked about that right off. How are they doing? Is she still hanging on?

Freddy: Yes, but her doctors are saying a week to ten days. He's not taking it well. It's not like it's a surprise—we all knew this was coming—but he's coming unhinged. I don't think I can let him be alone. I've pretty much resigned myself to coming with him and staying a few weeks. Long enough anyway until he figures out what he wants to do. I'm getting things in order here at the restaurant for us to both be away for a stretch.

Ben was Freddy's best friend, had been since they were kids. He was the only person—besides Adam, temporarily—

who'd seen through his rough exterior. And in Ben's case, that was because he shared it. He'd had it worse than Freddy, actually, in that he'd essentially been left to fend for himself as a kid. At least Freddy'd had his mom and Sophie.

To Freddy's mind, there were two kinds of people in the world: people who stuck by you no matter what and people who didn't. Ben was in the former category and, as such, had earned Freddy's fierce loyalty.

And now Ben's wife was dying. And after she did, he was determined to head back to the town of their youth and hole up for a while.

Which meant Freddy was, too.

In Freddy's opinion, Ben was idealizing the place. Freddy and Ben had left Bishop's Glen together, exchanging their dishwasher and busboy jobs for similarly shitty jobs in New York City. But the difference was that in New York, there was room to climb the ladder. Bishop's Glen had rich people and poor people and very few people in between. You either owned a vineyard or a summer place or you worked in the service industry waiting on those people and on the tourists who came to visit the wineries.

In New York, no one knew Freddy. No one looked at him and dismissed him out of hand as a result of some kind of bullshit small-town groupthink.

The gamble had paid off. After a few years in New York, both he and Ben had worked their way into progressively more senior kitchen jobs. And when they took the big leap and opened their own place with the backing of a couple of loyal, deep-pocketed customers, they'd found success beyond their wildest dreams.

That would not have happened back in the armpit of the

Finger Lakes. If he had stayed in Bishop's Glen, Freddy would still be washing dishes.

But Ben was a nicer person than Freddy was. Where Freddy had ruthlessly cut out the cancer that was his past, Ben, even in those early, heady, New York City years, had waxed nostalgic about the town of their youth. The lake, the falling-down town square that was supposedly haunted by the ghost of its founder, the bush parties—it all seemed to have a pull on him. Once the money from their Food Network show started rolling in, Ben had bought a place on the lake. And now that his beloved wife was dying, hooked up to a state-of-the-art hospital bed in Manhattan, the only thing getting him through was the prospect of "heading home," of sitting on the deck at the lake, staring into the sunset, and letting his grief subsume him. It was like he thought the lake had magical fucking healing powers.

Sophie: Well, I'm glad I'm back in town. I can help Ben, maybe—if he wants me to. And the circumstances are terrible, but I'll be happy to see you without having to drag my ass to NYC.

Freddy: I'll be happy to see you, too. So what'd you buy? Does it come with a wine slushie machine?

Sophie: Kellynch Estates.

Freddy's phone and his glass of whiskey both clattered to the pavement.

Sophie had bought *Kellynch*?

Of course she had. Because that was just his luck. That fucking town had it in for him.

There was probably an "of all the wine joints in the world" joke to be made here, but he couldn't fight his way through the panic that was descending to make it.

But no. No panic. He needed to tamp that shit down. He was long past expending emotional energy over the inhabitants of Kellynch. He forced himself to focus. Stooped to pick up the phone, cursing the shaking of his hands—he *hated* it when his body lagged behind his brain. The screen had cracked—*shit*.

Sophie was still texting.

Sophie: Kellynch is a little ways out of town, and it was never one of the big players, so you probably don't know it.

Oh, he knew it.

Knew exactly how far out of town it was—a thirty-five minute walk on his own, closer to fifty with Adam. Knew all the private nooks and crannies of those outbuildings his sister had been raving about. Knew how cold the water was when you dipped into the lake after dark.

Knew ways to warm up inside that lake, too.

Fuck.

No. He wasn't letting his mind go there.

Sophie: I had only vaguely heard the name. It was owned by a family called Elliot, and I do kind of remember the Elliot siblings even though I think they were all younger than I was. Anyway, it wasn't one of the

21

places we used to clean. And I don't know if there's a slushie machine! These foreclosure auctions move fast. You just kind of have to jump without really getting a detailed look at the place. But Freddy, it's lovely. I adore it.

He tried out the phone. It still worked despite the crack. Not unlike his heart.

Freddy: What happened to the Elliots?

He immediately regretted the question. Why ask a question when you didn't care about the answer? Hadn't he just reminded himself that he was done expending energy on this topic?

Sophie: I don't really know. The last family winemaker died a few years ago. I guess they couldn't keep it going?

The last family winemaker would have been Adam's dad—since he never let Adam in on the business.

Poor Adam, left with only his crazy mother and siblings. Even though he'd been pretty distant with Adam, his dad had always been the sane one. Relatively speaking, anyway.

But no. There was no Poor Adam. Adam didn't need—or deserve—Freddy's pity. Freddy ordered himself to have some fucking pride and *stop* thinking about Adam.

Sophie: They apparently had someone in on contract after that, but it didn't work out.

The last harvest was several years ago now. That's all I know, really. Somehow it ended up with them losing everything. I feel a little bad taking someone's house under such sad circumstances.

This should be good news. The part of Freddy that was reveling in the idea of Sophie sitting on her porch and looking down her nose at all the snobs in that town should be doing a dance of joy. If there was a little bit of poetic justice in Sophie returning to Bishop's Glen as a home- and business-owner, there was *shit-ton* of it in her doing so at Kellynch Estates specifically. The Elliots were getting what was coming to them.

So it was fine. He would make his visit as short as he could manage, and he'd stay with Ben. Or hell, maybe he'd stay at one of those fucking B and Bs they used to clean. As soon as he was assured that Ben was going to be okay, he'd hightail it out of there.

It's fine, he told himself again.

He blew some dirt off his damaged phone and took a deep breath to calm his roiling guts.

It did not feel fine.

CHAPTER THREE

Eight years ago

The first time Freddy laid eyes on Adam, he fell in love a little bit.

Or so he assumed, being unfamiliar with the emotion. He could only speculate what this strange jolt was. It felt like interest, but more. Lust, but more. The physical sensations cascading through his body—shortened breaths, jumpy limbs, a fluttery stomach—were not unprecedented, but in the past, they had heralded anger. Fear. Self-preservation. These were the things he felt when he had to defend himself—when he was younger from actual physical blows on the playground and now from the more subtle but just as insidious slurs about his appearance, his lack of a father, his poverty—you name it.

But he wasn't angry right now, at least not any more than usual. No, he'd just been standing outside Miller's Inn having a cigarette before his shift started when Adam came limping up to the valet stand and kept on going right into Freddy's heart.

He'd looked up, caught Freddy's eye, and flashed a crooked smile. Then, seeming to think better of it, he'd looked at the ground, quickly, almost like he was embarrassed.

It was awfully fucking cute.

"Hey." Freddy nodded at another member of the kitchen staff, a cook who had just appeared for a smoke break. "Who's the new guy?" He tried to pitch the question so it came out sounding like he was merely mildly interested.

"New valet, you mean?"

"Yeah."

"That's Adam Elliot."

Freddy didn't know the name, but that wasn't saying much. He wasn't very well connected in Bishop's Glen—by design. He kept his head down. Had little interest in being social with these people, with the exception of his friend Ben Captain.

"Adam Elliot," he echoed, savoring the feeling of the name in his mouth. "What's his deal?"

"His family owns Kellynch Estates."

Shit. That must be one of the wineries around town. So this guy was definitely from the other side of the proverbial tracks. "Why's he working here, then?"

"Beats me." His colleague stubbed out his cigarette and said, "See you."

Freddy took a long, slow drag of his own cancer stick and ordered himself to get his shit together. To assess the situation logically. What was it about this guy that had done such a number on him?

He was of average height—shorter than Freddy—and kind of small-boned. He had slightly wavy dark brown hair and pale skin. He looked almost otherworldly—or he would have if he hadn't been wearing the standard valet uniform of a Miller's Inn–branded polo shirt and black pants.

None of it added up. There was no rational reason for Freddy to be so...compelled by this guy.

And then, just as he was talking himself out of this stupid crush, Adam Elliot lifted his head and looked right at Freddy again.

And smiled.

And this time, he sustained it. It was a big, guileless, almost goofy smile.

And Freddy was undone.

Present day

Just before dawn the day after packing up the library, Adam emerged from underneath his RV, wiped his fingers on his coveralls, and crossed them. The vehicle, which had already been old when he bought it, had only ever been driven once in the years he owned it, and that had been onto the site on the vineyard where it was currently parked.

It was fine inside. Roomy, as far as these things went, and well organized—it was a Class-A RV the previous owners had basically never used. And since he used it as a stationary living space, he hadn't much concerned himself with the health of its engine.

It had been parked here between Kellynch's southernmost stand of vines and the surrounding forest for several years, since he'd moved out of the house. He had concentrated all his energy on incrementally transforming the interior, but he probably should have taken it for a spin every now and then. It wasn't like he couldn't have foreseen a day when, left to run unchecked by Dad, his mother's profligacy would mean saying goodbye to Kellynch. But what do they say about the shoemaker's children going shoeless?

A twig snapped, and Mr. Collins went bananas.

"Shut up," he said to the mutt, but he pulled out his Remington 700 all the same. There were coyotes in these woods, and Mr. Collins, although his sense of himself was large, was no bigger than a shoebox—not to mention as dumb as one and therefore all the more likely to end up a coyote's breakfast if Adam wasn't vigilant.

"Holy mother of God! Put that thing down! It's just me!"

"Rusty." Adam's employer—and best friend—stepped into the circle of illumination cast by the work light Adam had set up. Adam set aside the ancient hunting rifle. "Or should I say Lady Merlot?"

Rusty was in his drag persona, Lady Rusty Merlot, a winedrinking, ratchet-wielding queen who combined Rusty's real life callings: fixing cars and drinking wine. Lady Merlot's most popular number, in fact, was a mash-up of "Red Red Wine" and "Little Red Corvette."

"Did you come right from Whine?" The bar Rusty performed in was two doors down from his automotive shop, so it was easy enough to go home and change before continuing to another destination, but Rusty enjoyed raising eyebrows and as such seized any opportunity to wander through the wider world as Lady Merlot.

"What do you think?" Lady Merlot twirled, making her deep red velvet dress—Rusty and Lady Merlot were nothing if not consistent with their brand—flare up. "When you texted last night that you were leaving the great resurrection to this morning, I thought, *I simply cannot miss this*." Lady Merlot held up both hands. In one was a toolbox; in the other, a bottle of wine. "I also thought you might need some help."

Adam chuckled. "It's a little early for me."

"No, darling. It's late. You just need to change your perspective on things—one of these days you'll actually listen to me when I tell you that."

I did listen, though. I listened when it mattered the most.

But that wasn't fair, as he was forever reminding himself. He'd been nineteen when he turned his back on Freddy. Old enough to know his own mind.

"Hello, you ugly beast." Lady Merlot bent down to pet Mr. Collins. Mr. Collins was so stupid, he didn't seem to understand that Lady Merlot and Rusty were the same person. The mutt was indifferent to Rusty, which was weird because he liked most people, but he adored Lady Merlot—as evidenced by how enthusiastically he was licking her face.

"Just give him a gentle shove, and he'll leave you alone."

"Are you kidding me?" Lady Merlot dropped the toolbox she was carrying and gave Mr. Collins a squeeze. "I'm not as young as I used to be. I gotta take it where I can get it."

Adam glanced at the toolbox. "I don't think I'll need those, either. If this thing doesn't start, I'm not sure a ratchet and a screwdriver is going to make much of a difference."

"Which is why I also called Mikey Barnes in Auburn. He can get a fifty-ton rotator down here by eight and tow you out if need be."

And that right there exemplified Rusty. He could be a pain in the ass a lot of the time, but he cared about Adam. He had since the first day they met, when, as a seventeen-year-old closet case, Adam had "happened" into Whine with a fake ID on a night Rusty was performing. Since then, Rusty had been a cross between a father figure and a best friend, training Adam as a mechanic and gently helping him face the fact that unless he worked up some courage, he was going to spend his entire life in the closet.

And when Adam had come out to his family a little later and his parents had freaked out and kicked him out for a while, it had been Rusty he'd run to. Rusty who'd let him sleep on his sofa. Rusty who'd spackled his frightened, broken heart back together.

Adam still remembered the visceral terror of those days, of being suddenly and ruthlessly cut loose from everything and everyone he'd known. Of being not just an orphan in the sense of facing the loss of his family, but of being placeless. A person without a place.

Adam belonged at Kellynch. He was of it. Like it had birthed him. His earliest memories were of lying among the vines, looking at the sky. In those *Masterpiece Theatre*–type dramas they always said the name of the house after the person, and it felt like that applied to him. Adam Elliot of Kellynch Estates.

What did you become if you were of a place and you lost that place?

But Rusty had stabilized him. Dried his tears. Cursed his family. Forced him to keep putting one foot in front of the other. He'd given Adam a part-time job, paying him to keep the shop tidy and gradually teaching him to fix cars.

The funny thing about Adam's break with his family was that it seemed to affect Rusty as much as it had Adam. Rusty always used to talk vaguely about "the future" when Adam was no longer in Bishop's Glen. He'd worked up a notion that Adam was "too good" for the town, and that he'd save up a bit of money working at the shop and then go somewhere else for college. He never listened when Adam protested that he *liked* Bishop's Glen and had no desire to leave.

After all the drama, Adam's family had actually come around pretty quickly. His siblings, bless them, were of the generation for whom homosexuality didn't register as a big deal. His parents had eventually...softened. Not apologized exactly, but suggested that Adam should come home. And then they'd never talked about it again, except for the odd reference from his mother to "the gay thing," which was usually in the context of her listing his faults.

So Adam had moved back home. It was better to have a family than not have one. It was better to be at Kellynch than not be at Kellynch, even though his dad never let him do anything beyond help with the harvest, which was a time they needed all hands on deck.

Adam had done other stuff, though—repairing barrels, taking in the dock in the winter, re-graveling the drive when it needed it. After he had moved back home from Rusty's, he'd been seized with the desire to be good. To do his duty and make himself useful to his family—and the only way he'd really known to do that was with handyman stuff.

His dad had only been forty-six, and he'd been in good health—they'd thought. Adam had somehow thought he had more time. That maybe he could quietly, incrementally prove himself. That with the passage of time, his dad would come to see that of his three kids, Adam was the one who loved Kellynch the most.

"Or," Rusty said, breaking into Adam's reverie, "We can get Mikey to tow this monster somewhere else entirely. Rochester, maybe."

Here they went. Even though Adam had forgiven his family for casting him out—it had been the price of coming home to Kellynch—Rusty never really had. And in some ways, he'd never really forgiven *Adam* for not leaving town.

Adam frequently reminded himself that Rusty meant well. Even though Rusty often got it wrong, he was the only person in Bishop's Glen who knew the real Adam. The only person who advocated for him. Who arranged for a giant-ass tow truck when Adam needed one. And that wasn't nothing.

He made a noncommittal noise in response to Rusty's suggestion that he have the RV towed out of town. As with Adam's mother, the path of least resistance with Rusty was usually to just let him talk.

Rusty rose from petting Mr. Collins and eyed the RV. "So when do you have to be out of here, and why didn't you do this yesterday?"

Adam sighed and looked at his watch. "Six, and I just…ran out of steam last night." Packing the library had turned into a surprisingly maudlin exercise. After he'd finished, he'd returned to his pinot and allowed himself, for the first time, really, to wallow. To truly let it sink in that all his father's work, and his grandmother's, had come to nothing.

Unfortunately, the proverbial "life is short" lesson his dad's death had brought had come too late to really make a difference. Why hadn't he outright asked his dad for more responsibility? Why had he assumed that with enough time, they'd come around? He should have made his case for what he wanted, clearly and without equivocation.

Anyway, it was all water under the bridge now. Wine down the drain.

"All right." Rusty stood and slapped the side of the RV. "Let's try and start him." Rusty, in contrast to probably every other mechanic everywhere, gave cars male pronouns. It still made Adam smile, all these years later.

Adam got himself settled, stuck the key in the ignition, and turned it.

Some wheezing occurred.

"Come on, pretty boy!" Rusty said.

The engine turned over, and Rusty cheered. "Do you even have a license for this thing?"

"You don't need a license for an RV." You did, however, need a special endorsement on your license to drive one of this size in New York State, but he'd never bothered getting one since he'd always planned on ignoring the *mobile* part of his mobile home. "Anyway, I'm only going to Mark's."

"Mark's." Rusty curled his lip. It was a mannerism of his, one that was amusingly similar to one of Adam's mother's. As much as Rusty did not approve of Wilhelmina—and vice-versa —they were both masters of conveying disapproval nonverbally.

Mark's place was about as far from "leaving town" as Adam could get. Rusty would view it as a step backward— which on the surface of things, it probably was. Adam was going from living in his RV on the spacious grounds of Kellynch to parking it in his little brother's backyard.

"I know you won't listen to me," Rusty said, "but you know you can park this at the shop until you decide your next move."

"I appreciate it, but I'm good at Mark's, for now at least." What Rusty didn't understand was that, as much as it made Adam sound like a Boy Scout, he needed nature in his life. It was going to be hard enough to leave the protective embrace of the vines at Kellynch. Setting up in the asphalt jungle of the auto shop, which was located on the outskirts of downtown in a strip of light industry, dive bars, and boarded-up buildings, did not appeal at all. Mark had a small house, but a big backyard.

"Well," said Rusty, "you're going to make quite the splash in Uppercross."

"I know, right?" Adam did a jazz-hands gesture. "The gimpy queer brother in the RV is here!"

Rusty rolled his eyes. "I'm surprised they went for it."

"It turns out, as status-conscious as they are, the prospect of free childcare onsite was too much to pass up. They did try to get me to leave the RV and move into their basement, though."

"I might not even argue with that. Mark and Chloe's place isn't ideal, but at least it doesn't have wheels." Rusty did the lip-curling thing again.

Adam reached out the open driver's side window and patted the side of the RV. As he got older, it was kind of...fun to defy Rusty. Maybe he was having a belated adolescent rebellious phase—against a drag queen mechanic instead of his actual family. "Hey, I love this place. It's plenty big enough, and it's all mine." All paid for, too. Once the writing was on the wall for Kellynch, Adam had given some thought to buying a small place in town, but he didn't want to take on a mortgage. He was allergic to debt, basically. So, yeah, he was moving in with his little brother, but it was his best option at the moment, given his priorities.

"Can I give you a lift?" he asked Rusty.

"Sure. But only because it's early enough that no one will see me in this hideous thing."

"Walk around and pull the steps up when you close the door, will you?"

After Rusty got settled in the passenger seat, Adam pressed his foot down slowly on the gas, and the RV eased into motion. He had to swallow a lump in his throat as he maneuvered past the vines.

"And we're off," Rusty said as they pulled onto the road. "On to bigger and better things."

Bigger and better things.

Adam could not agree with that assessment. He was happy to have a short break from his mom and Betsy, but without Kellynch, he was pretty sure life was going to be, well, small and worse.

He forced himself not to look in the side mirror as he drove away from Kellynch for the last time.

CHAPTER FOUR

Eight years ago

"Hey! Adam!"

Adam stopped and peered into the window of the ancient, rusty Mustang that had pulled up next to him on the deserted road. It was that guy from work—Freddy Wentworth.

Freddy was twenty-one years old. Worked during the week at the Bee's Knees and on weekends at Miller's Inn, where his mom cleaned rooms. Allegedly the son of a migrant worker his mother had hooked up with. Known for his tom-catting ways and his propensity for swearing and smoking and just generally getting into trouble. He'd dropped out of high school when he was a junior, so Adam hadn't overlapped with him there.

It was possible that Adam had asked around a bit about Freddy Wentworth.

What he hadn't had to ask about, because he could see them with his own eyes, were Freddy's sunny good looks, which were so at odds with his persona. Freddy put the car in park, leaned across the center console of his car, and speared Adam with an intense look. It was dark, but Adam knew those eyes were an impossibly deep blue, topped by thick, fair eyebrows. His clean-shaven jaw, which was also sort of at odds with his bad-boy image, was lit up by the dashboard lights. It was strong and angular and...hard to stop looking at.

"You still walking everywhere?" His lips quirked into a grin.

"Yup." Adam's lips did the same thing. It was like Freddy's face had some kind of magnetic force in it that made Adam's copy its expressions.

Freddy had been offering Adam rides home after work the last few weekends, and Adam had been declining, though he wasn't sure why. Probably out of self-preservation. Freddy Wentworth was gorgeous enough, and compelling enough, to make Adam consider abandoning his commitment to pedestrianism. Which was exactly why he was hesitant. He was crushing pretty hard on Freddy, but he was smart enough to know that no good could ever come of it. Freddy, a full-fledged adult, and a bit of a wild one at that, was out his league.

"A mechanic who walks everywhere. It's kind of funny."

Adam shrugged. "I like to fix cars more than drive them, I guess."

"Why?"

Adam had always loved to walk, even if he did sometimes pay for it later with pain and the need for more downtime. There was something meditative about walking, especially when his wanderings took him into his beloved woods. It got him away from all the critical voices in his head—including his own. But that would sound dumb to someone as cool as Freddy, so instead of answering the *why do you like to walk?* part of the question, he decided to address the *why do you like to fix cars?* part. "Cars are like puzzles." He thought of his mother ragging him earlier today about getting his freckles bleached and Rusty doing the same yesterday about his leaving town. Speaking of critical voices... He smiled. "Also, cars don't talk back."

Freddy cocked his head, looked like he was going to say something more. Adam held his breath. But why? What mysterious thing could Adam be wanting to hear? Freddy to force him to accept a ride?

Maybe they could just...chat. That had been happening lately, too. Freddy had been stopping by the valet stand on his way in for his shift, or on smoke breaks, to shoot the breeze. They talked about cars, mostly, once Freddy found out that Adam's full-time job was working at Anderson Motors.

In the end, though, Freddy didn't say anything. After staring at Adam for a few moments, he winked, said "You be careful," and *vroomed* away.

Present day

"Uhh, Adam. I am *so* sick."

Adam's brother, Mark, was lying on the sofa with his eyes closed when Adam came into the house. Mark had his phone in one hand, though, and it was open to Facebook.

Mark's wife, Chloe, looked up from her own phone and rolled her eyes. "Try hungover."

"Adam!" Adam's niece and nephew greeted him in their customary fashion, hurling themselves at his legs. He'd been living in his RV in the backyard for two weeks now, and the kids were in heaven. They were his biggest fans. Well, they were pretty much his *only* fans, but they made up for it with the extremeness of their devotion.

"Hi, munchkins." He picked up four-year-old Mark Jr. and ruffled six-year-old Whitney's hair.

Mark sneezed in his face.

"Mark Jr., on the other hand, is *actually* sick," Chloe said. Before Adam could reply, she was on her feet, looking out the living room window at the street. "There's the Escalade." She heaved a put-upon sigh that reminded him of his mother's, which was funny because Chloe and Wilhelmina were related only by marriage.

"Parking right in front of our house, I suppose." Even though Mark's eyes were closed, Adam was pretty sure they were rolling.

"Where else?" Chloe tapped her fingernails on the window.

"Are Henry and Lulu *ever* going to move out?" Mark asked.

Adam's brother and sister-in-law had a frenemies sort of relationship with their neighbors across the street, the McGuires. They had all gone to high school with the McGuire kids, Henry and Lulu, who still lived in their parents' house despite the fact that they were in their late twenties. Lulu and Henry had been popular at school, and they still were among the townspeople. As far as Adam could tell, that popularity was merited. Both siblings were fun-loving and likable—not that Mark and Chloe saw it that way.

Uppercross was a mixture of modest old bungalows like Mark and Chloe's and newer McMansions built when their owners bought a bungalow, tore it down, and built a new house in its place. The McGuires fell into the latter category, and Mark and Chloe hated them for it. Not because they hated their house, as Adam did, but because they resented their wealth. To Mark and Chloe, everything was a zero-sum-game. If the McGuires were doing well, it must be at Mark and Chloe's expense.

"It's not enough that they have to have *four* cars, they have to park them right in front of our house?" The McGuires' fleet of luxury cars was an evergreen source of suffering for Mark and Chloe.

"It's not like you're using the spot." Adam didn't know why he was trying to reason with them. "And it's a public street."

"Yes, but they're just flaunting it, parking it right there," Mark said.

Adam was sure the McGuires, who, despite their ugly-ass house, were nice people who'd been nothing but kind to Mark and Chloe, hadn't thought of it in those terms at all. He was tempted to suggest that Mark and Chloe stop interpreting everyone's actions as being about them. Still, he was practical —you had to be with his family—so he left it alone.

"Anyway," Chloe said to her husband, "since you're hungover, I'm assuming you won't be going to the bush party tonight." She turned to Adam. "You should come with me."

"I'm not hungover," Mark said. "I'm *sick*."

"Whatever."

"Thanks," Adam said to Chloe, "but I think I'll take a pass." Bishop's Glen had a pretty well-established bush-party scene. The town's young people would head out into a forest clearing or a fallow farm field with cheap local wine and the makings of a bonfire and sit around and drink. He'd gone sometimes when he was younger, but he'd never really been that comfortable at parties. He'd long since grown out of them. Mark and Chloe had not.

"I wonder if the McGuires are going." Chloe was still

scowling out the window. "It's going to be a big crowd tonight because Freddy Wentworth is in town."

Adam almost dropped his nephew as adrenaline erupted inside him. He had to force himself to lower the boy with arms that suddenly felt made of jelly. "I'm sorry, *what?*"

"Freddy Wentworth." Chloe must have mistaken Adam's shock for confusion, because she added, "You know. The Food Network chef? That show *Food Fanatics* where he goes around and eats food and gets mad at people for making it wrong? And that Ben Captain guy follows him around trying to smooth things over?"

Oh, Adam knew the show. He had every single one of its twenty-two-episode run saved on his DVR. Sometimes at night, God help him, he turned it on, closed his eyes, and let Freddy talk him to sleep. *You call this a roux? Here, let me show you, you idiot.* It was surreal, not least because the Freddy Adam had known had been nothing but kind. Gentle.

"He was a big troublemaker when we were kids?" Chloe was still trying to jog Adam's memory. "Greaser type? You probably don't remember him because he was a bit older."

"Oh, Adam knows Freddy," Mark said. "They were friends for a while."

"*Really?*" Chloe was surprised. Everyone had been. On paper it had been an odd friendship. In reality, it had been the most natural thing in the world—and it had been more than a friendship. "Then you *have* to come."

Adam made fists to try to stop his hands from shaking. He shouldn't be so gobsmacked. Freddy's sister had bought Kellynch—that *had* been a shock, and one he was still reeling from. He hadn't recognized her married name when he'd learned the identity of the purchasers. It had only been a week ago, when she'd moved to town and tongues had started wagging, that he'd made the connection. But given that Sophie *had* bought Kellynch, why was Adam so surprised that Freddy might come to town to visit her?

Mark sat up. "You know what? I'm starting to feel much better."

"You two go." Adam forced himself to slow his breathing so he could talk like a normal person. "I'll stay with the munchkins." He never minded hanging with Whitney and Mark Jr. And now? If it meant not going to a party at which Freddy Wentworth would be in attendance? Not only did he not mind, he *insisted*.

"Oh, I don't think we can possibly ask you to babysit again," said Chloe in a manner that suggested she was thinking of exactly that.

"But we're gonna work on the playhouse!" Whitney exclaimed.

Yes. Saved by the six-year-old. He was building the kids a playhouse out back, and the next task was to add the roof.

"Okay, but since Mark is sick"—Chloe shot her husband a look—"I'm going to send him home early to swap with you, and then you can come. He should get to bed early, and you should get to say hi to Freddy."

"Sure." Adam only agreed because he knew that once the partying started, she would forget about him. People generally did.

They left, and that was that. Adam and the kids ate some mac and cheese. They made a playhouse roof out of one-by-fours. They watched some *PAW Patrol*. A normal, unremarkable Saturday night.

Except for the fact that *Freddy Wentworth* was less than five miles away.

It was like Adam could *feel* him. Well, no, what he was

feeling was more like imaginary bugs crawling under his skin, making him jumpy and agitated. Freddy, back in the day, had made him agitated, but in a much more enjoyable way. He could close his eyes and be back in the lake, shivering from a mixture of cold and lust as Freddy's hands roamed all over his body.

It was hard to square that version of Freddy, the one who, gilded with moonlight, had whispered words of affection into Adam's ear, with the TV version of Freddy, who yelled and cursed and banged pots around. But then, Adam had always seen a different side of Freddy. A private version Freddy didn't show to anyone else. Adam wondered if that Freddy still existed, or if Adam, by breaking his heart, had killed him off.

The worst part about it was the knowledge that Rusty had been wrong about Freddy. Totally, utterly wrong. Contrary to Rusty's predictions, Freddy had made something of himself. He was the town's most famous export. His New York restaurant had a two-month waiting list for a table, and his Food Network show had been a huge hit, catapulting him and his friend Ben into the ranks of celebrity chefs.

No, the *worst* part was that some part of Adam had known, even back then, that Rusty was wrong. He'd known Freddy would make something of himself. Or at least he'd known it didn't matter. That his essential nature—his Freddyness—was enough. Was everything.

He had known all that, and still he'd let himself be persuaded.

This wasn't so bad. Freddy took in the familiar surroundings of a Bishop's Glen bush party. If he had to think back to one thing about the town of his youth he *didn't* hate, it might be a bush party. You could see the stars out here, which was something he hadn't even realized he'd missed. And the smell. In the summer, the rural and forested land around the town smelled…green. Intensely, gorgeously *green*. There was no other word for it. Plants at the peak of their life cycles, full of stored energy, bursting with life and potential. You didn't get that in New York City.

There was quite a crowd out tonight, and an older one than he remembered. There were lots of people here he'd overlapped with in school, and he was twenty-nine. He recognized everyone from the former high school quarterback to the guy he'd washed dishes with at the Bee's Knees. For some reason, these parties had always drawn from across the social spectrum. Kids of rich residents and kids like him. They'd drink local plonk and cook over the fire. In all his years of Michelin-starred cooking and dining, he'd never tasted anything quite like a spicy pork sausage from Ken Rawlings's farm roasted over an open fire. And despite having a sommelier's course under his belt, he still had a secret soft spot for room-temperature Riesling that wasn't nearly as acidic as it should be.

"Don't hog Freddy, Henry."

Lulu McGuire appeared, hands on hips, silhouetted against the bonfire behind her.

He almost laughed. There was another thing that hadn't changed. Lulu McGuire had been the homecoming queen back in the day, the peak of the social pyramid in high school—and judging by the way people deferred to her, she still was.

She tried to edge in between her brother Henry and Freddy, who were sitting on a log. That *was* something new. Lulu McGuire hadn't paid much attention to him back in the day, at bush parties or elsewhere. She hadn't been cruel like most people. Lulu had always been a nice girl, if not the brightest bulb. She'd just been busy with her friends, and Freddy had not been one of those.

Freddy hadn't had any friends besides Ben, actually, unless you counted that summer with Adam, and he *didn't*.

"He's not a *blanket*, Lulu." Henry stood—or sat—his ground on the log next to Freddy. "He's a person. He can't be *hogged*."

And *that* was something different, too. Last time Freddy paid any attention to Henry McGuire, who was a couple years younger than Lulu and him, the guy had been straight. Or so Freddy had presumed. Judging by the all the flirting and the suggestive looks Henry was throwing Freddy's way this evening, that was no longer the case.

Lulu huffed and came around to sit on Freddy's other side. "Freddy. We were all so *shocked* when you came out on TV as bisexual. I mean, I knew you were into guys, but I had *no idea* you liked girls, too."

That's because Lulu had never paid any attention to him. Yes, his big Bishop's Glen outing had involved that ill-advised blow job that had made him infamous in town, but he'd fooled around with both boys and girls in his youth and had never tried to hide that fact. And he'd fooled around *a lot*—before Adam, anyway. Funnily enough, even though everyone looked down on him, he'd never really had much trouble rustling up a certain kind of companionship when he'd wanted it.

Ironically, the only thing he'd ever been in the closet about was the one time he actually fell in love.

Henry scooched a little closer to Freddy. "Was that planned? I've always heard those shows are actually scripted."

"It wasn't planned." Freddy tried to think back to the episode in question. It had been a throwaway remark, something he'd said in response to a homophobic statement made by a chef whose restaurant the show was visiting. It had just been a little "fuck you," which he'd thought had gone with his TV persona. The persona itself *had* been kind of scripted. They'd wanted him to be the cranky, foul-mouthed bad boy— the bad cop to Ben's good cop. It wasn't a huge leap—they merely wanted an exaggerated version of his real self. He'd been happy to oblige. He *was* kind of an asshole, and the show had really been Ben's thing.

He'd been surprised when his offhand "I'm bisexual, so stop with this bullshit" comment had garnered a landslide of "celebrity chef comes out" media attention. It was funny that in Bishop's Glen, everyone thought he was gay, but in the wider world, he was assumed to be straight. So in a way, pronouncing himself bi on national TV had amounted to coming out in both directions to both audiences.

The resulting media firestorm had passed quickly, though, and for a while, it had gotten him *a lot* of extra attention of the male variety, which was not something Freddy had minded.

Lulu scooted a little closer to Freddy from the other side. They were gradually smushing him in the middle of a McGuire sandwich. Then she leaned forward and glared at her brother around Freddy's torso. Freddy almost laughed. Had he ever imagined being the object of interest of one of the McGuire siblings, much less both?

He should probably be more annoyed by it. Take his own advice to Sophie about looking down his nose at all the bastards in this town, but the truth was the McGuires had always been pleasant, if a bit shallow. And the other, more immediate truth was that they'd both grown up quite nicely.

Lulu still had the blinding smile and killer curves that had gotten her elected homecoming queen, and Henry, who had been a wiry soccer star in high school, had bulked out considerably. He was wearing a tight tank top that showed off arms and shoulders honed to perfection.

Maybe this little sojourn in Bishop's Glen wouldn't be totally without its amusements. Freddy got so busy in New York that he rarely made time for anything beyond a quick hookup. Customers frequently came on to him, and when he had the inclination, he took one home. The catch was that he usually didn't have the time.

But now, here, with Ben lost in grief and Freddy refusing to abandon him, he had nothing *but* time.

"Hey, now," he said to both McGuires. "There's enough room for everyone."

"Oh, but here comes Adam Elliot," Lulu said. "He'll need to sit down. Get up, Henry."

And just like that, *Adam Fucking Elliot* walked into the circle of light cast by the fire. Freddy's body started doing that thing where it refused to get the *be cool* message his mind was sending. Thousands of tiny pins were pricking his skin, and someone had turned the temperature up on the fire from pleasantly toasty to hellish inferno.

Adam still had the same limp that created his signature loping gait. Still had that dark, wavy hair, that light dusting of freckles over delicate facial bones. He was wearing a pair of faded jeans and a snug-fitting T-shirt, but Freddy suspected that unlike Henry, Adam wasn't doing it on purpose. Adam wasn't vain.

Although, how did he know that? Everything he'd thought he'd known about Adam had been a lie, hadn't it?

Adam didn't notice Freddy at first. His sister-in-law, Chloe, greeted him, and they had a conversation about whether Mark, who had been at the party earlier but had apparently gone home, was going to let the kids stay up too late.

The longer Adam stood there without seeing him, the more uncomfortable Freddy got. He realized he'd been holding his breath, so he stopped—but that resulted in an audible, sharp exhale that drew the attention of Lulu next to him.

"Hey, Adam!" she called. "You remember Freddy Wentworth? Our resident famous person has returned to the fold!"

"Temporarily returned." Freddy congratulated himself that his voice had come out sounding even and unbothered.

"Yeah." Adam nodded at him like you'd nod at someone you vaguely remembered from your past. "I was sorry to hear about Ben Captain's wife. I knew her a little—she had major car troubles a couple years ago when she and Ben were here for a few weeks, so she saw more of me than she probably wanted to. But she was always gracious."

"You still fix cars?" Freddy asked. Amazingly, he continued to sound undisturbed.

"Oh, yeah," Henry said. "Adam works his magic at Anderson Motors. You remember Rusty Anderson?"

Freddy sure as hell did. The old queen had taken way too much interest in Adam back in the day, in Freddy's opinion. Had too much sway over him.

"There's not a car they can't fix between the pair of them," Henry said.

Adam looked at the ground. Was he blushing? There was nothing to indicate that—the light of the fire wasn't bright enough to illuminate subtle changes in skin tone. But Adam had always flushed easily, and Freddy knew that mannerism. Adam had always looked at the ground and sort of done a half smile when he was embarrassed—and he had always been so delightfully easy to tease into a blush.

Freddy wondered what had inspired this one. Was he embarrassed that he was still in Bishop's Glen fixing cars? If the Elliots had lost Kellynch to foreclosure, things probably weren't going too well. He hoped that at least—

No. Adam was not his problem anymore. He didn't wish him ill, but he wasn't going to waste any time feeling sorry for him. Hoping for some outcome or other. Hope was an utterly useless emotion, in matters of the heart and in life more generally. Things either happened or they didn't. Hope had no bearing on the matter. Hard work, maybe, if you were looking for an avenue of influence, but not hope. Hope was for the weak-willed.

"And, oh!" Henry exclaimed. "Freddy, it just occurred to me that your sister now owns—"

"Shh!" Lulu shot her brother a death glare. Then, when no one said anything, she said, "Well, *that's* awkward."

"It's okay," Adam said quietly. "I was glad Kellynch went to someone like Sophie."

"You should sit," Freddy said to Adam. He rose, vacating his spot between the McGuire siblings. Adam hated being coddled—or at least he used to—but there was no reason for him to stand on that bad leg. It had always bothered him less when he was sitting or, somewhat counterintuitively, when he was walking. Walking took his mind off things, he'd always said.

And anyway, Freddy needed to leave. Needed this evening to be over. So he waved off Adam's protest and made his excuses to the group, promising Lulu and Henry that he would see them later in the week.

And that was that. He walked away from the fire and into the night toward his car.

When Freddy had thought about seeing Adam again—which he tried not to do, because he was done expending emotional energy on Adam Elliot—he imagined it being a Big Freaking Deal. There would be portentous music playing. The wind would be blowing. There might be yelling. Certainly, everyone would be staring at them.

He did not imagine it being so anticlimactic. *You still fix cars? Please, take my seat.* They could have been in one of those conversation-heavy costume dramas Adam always used to like to watch, the ones where all they did was talk and talk and talk and everyone was so emotionally stifled Freddy had always half expected one of the characters to suddenly snap and start doing whatever the nineteenth-century equivalent of going postal was.

Also: who was he kidding? He had *totally* thought about seeing Adam again.

But that was only because Adam had been his first love. People never forgot their first love, right? The sway Adam had over Freddy didn't have anything to do with Adam specifically. It was the *position* he held. His role. Surely if Adam himself still had any power over Freddy, that reunion would have been a lot different. There *would* have been portentous music and all that. The universe would have recognized it in some way as Monumental.

Right?

CHAPTER FIVE

Eight years ago

"Adam!"

Adam stopped. He knew that voice. Hell, he dreamed about that voice. It snaked through his subconscious while he slept, and he woke up with wet pajama bottoms.

It was like his ears were tuned to the exact frequency at which Freddy spoke. Like he had superhero abilities, supersonic hearing—but only for Freddy Wentworth.

What Adam didn't hear, along with Freddy's voice, was a car. Usually Freddy pulled up next to him, asked if he wanted a ride home, took Adam's *no thanks* in good stride, shot him a knee-dissolving grin, and took off.

He turned.

Freddy was jogging toward him.

"Where's your car?"

"Dead."

"Oh, crap!" Freddy lived on the other side of town—yes, Adam had investigated. It wasn't as far a walk as Kellynch, but most people weren't into freakishly long walks like Adam was. "What's wrong with it?"

Freddy made a *keep going* gesture and fell into step beside Adam. "I have no idea. The thing is so old, I'm not sure it's worth fixing anymore." He sighed. "The only thing I'm really pissed about is that I *just* filled that sucker with gas."

"You could siphon it out."

"Is that a thing people actually do? Outside of, like, the Great Depression?"

Adam cracked up. Freddy was so unexpectedly funny. When you looked at a guy like Freddy, you made certain assumptions. Adam was as guilty of it as anyone. Freddy looked like one of the guys from the movie *Grease*. He'd dropped out of school. But he had such a delightfully quick wit. He kind of reminded Adam of Rusty that way. Or of someone who would be in a drawing room in one of Jane Austen's novels—the slightly disrespectable guest who got by with a surfeit of charm.

"Can you get a tow? If so, why don't you bring it by Anderson Motors on Monday, and I'll have a look." He glanced over. By all accounts, Freddy and his family didn't have a lot of money. He didn't look poor, though. Well, he did look kind of raggedy—hair too long, jeans too ripped—but that seemed by design more than circumstance. He didn't want Freddy to think he considered him a charity case, but he added, "On the house. And if it's not an easy fix, I can at least get the gas out for you."

Freddy smiled like Adam had saved his drowning puppy. "That would be great—thanks." After a few more steps side by side, he asked, "So how come you work at Miller's if you have a full-time gig at Anderson?"

"Well, I only do the one shift a week at Miller's, on

Saturday nights, and it's mostly just to ogle the cars." Warmth spread through him when Freddy laughed. "I actually have a secret agenda," he confessed. He hadn't told anyone about it. His boss at Miller's would be pissed. Rusty he wasn't sure about. He might be pissed; he might proclaim Adam a brilliant schemer. But he'd decided not to test it because it would inevitably devolve into an argument about whether Adam should leave town.

"Yeah?"

"Well, so the owner of Anderson Motors is this guy Rusty Anderson."

"I know Rusty. Know of him anyway. He does drag, too, right? Over at Whine?"

Adam paused. He was almost certain Freddy was into guys but still found himself waiting for an expression of disgust or a hint of homosexual panic. This was a small, conservative town, and the topic of Rusty sometimes inspired unkind reactions. There was none of that with Freddy, though. "Yep. So Rusty is sort of like...a mentor to me."

"As it relates to cars," Freddy said, and Adam heard what he was really asking.

The weird thing about being out and being Adam Elliot was that the latter sometimes made people forget the former. Yes, he was out, but it was theoretical. He hadn't so much as kissed a guy. Or a girl, for that matter. Unlike Freddy, whose preferences had been effectively broadcast to the whole town when he'd been caught getting blown by a guy in public, Adam was quiet—almost painfully so. He liked books more than he liked most people. So there just weren't that many opportunities to tell people, or to remind people, that he was gay. So he had no idea if Freddy knew.

"Well, we're not a couple—he's too old for me. And also

just…not the type of guy I'd be into in that way." There. That would be enough to confirm his orientation. Adam congratulated himself on his casual delivery. "But Rusty is sort of a mentor in every other sense." Then he chuckled. "Well, not the drag thing. That's not my scene."

"I don't know." Freddy cocked his head. "You're good-looking enough."

And…wow. Adam flushed and looked at the ground—the pavement beneath their feet was suddenly extremely interesting.

The sensation of his cheeks heating was mortifying. His mother was always on him about his freckles or his hair, but honestly, if he could change one thing about himself, it would be the stupid blushing. He could only hope that the darkness —their walk was lit only by the moon and the occasional streetlight—prevented Freddy from seeing how much his compliment had affected Adam.

He cleared his throat. "Anyway, Rusty gave me a job when I really needed it. Gave me a place to stay, too, for a while, when I needed that. I…I've since patched things up enough with my family to move home, but basically I owe everything to Rusty. He's like…" How to explain Rusty? "He's a mentor, like I said, but he's also my best friend."

"You're lucky."

Adam nodded. He was. "So anyway, Rusty didn't really have enough business to hire me when I was in high school, but he did anyway. He let me answer phones and order parts and started teaching me about cars. It kind of gave me a purpose, you know? Got me out of the house, which…wasn't always the best place to be. Having a job gave me my own money. Then when I graduated last spring, he took me on full-time." Adam paused, wondering if he should say more. No.

There was no need for Freddy to know about the big blowup they'd had over the fact that Adam hadn't applied to any colleges. That the full-time offer was only for the summer because Rusty still expected Adam to get the hell out of Bishop's Glen, even without any college admission offers.

"But he still doesn't really have enough business to require a second mechanic full-time," Adam continued. "So what I do is..." He swiveled around. They had made their way out of the town proper and were on a deserted two-lane highway. He considered reminding Freddy that he was going the wrong way. That he should turn around and head back in the direction of his own home. But he didn't.

So, with one more glance to make sure no one was around to overhear, he lowered his voice and said, "I put business cards for Anderson Motors in the cars of the rich people who come to the inn."

"Ha!" Freddy's delighted bark of laughter echoed across the cool night, and it must have been contagious because Adam laughed, too. "The way you set that up, I thought you were going to confess something a lot more transgressive."

The fact that he'd confessed at all was pretty remarkable. Adam kept his cards close to his chest, usually. Rusty was the only person in the world he really trusted.

He'd thought.

"Yeah, so I got this stupid idea that if I could bring in some new business, I could earn my keep, so to speak."

"Not stupid," Freddy said. "Savvy. It bet it's working."

Adam grinned. "We did get a Mercedes in the other day that still had the card in the cup holder." He'd made sure to grab it before Rusty saw it.

Freddy raised a fist in triumph. "See?"

They'd reached the point where Adam turned from the

two-lane highway to a smaller road that would take him to the Kellynch driveway. "You should turn back. It's late."

"Eh, that's okay. I've come this far."

Adam gestured to his bum leg. "It's not much father to my place at normal speed, but we're moving slow."

Freddy shrugged. "I like slow. Slow lets you...savor things." He turned to Adam and winked, and suddenly Adam got the feeling that they were talking about more than just walking.

Present day

Adam had barely gotten over seeing Freddy at the bush party when it happened again. A week later, he was at one of Rusty's shows at Whine when Freddy arrived with the McGuire siblings.

And did he ever arrive with them—they were practically hanging off him, Lulu laughing uproariously and Henry sharing a knowing look with him like they had an inside joke. And it wasn't bad enough that Lulu, who generally made no pretense about her designs on rich and powerful men, was all over Freddy. No, he had to have the attention of Henry, too. Henry, who was objectively gorgeous.

The McGuires had always been nice to Adam, even back in high school when a lot of people razzed him about his limp. And Mark and Chloe's martyrdom aside, they were good neighbors to his brother and sister-in-law. Adam liked the McGuires.

He just didn't like them all over Freddy.

But then, he had no claim to Freddy. He'd forfeited that years ago.

"Hey, Adam. Can we join you?" Henry plopped down at Adam's table without waiting for an answer. Lulu and Freddy followed, Lulu greeting him enthusiastically, Freddy with a curt nod.

He still couldn't believe that Freddy was here. That they could occupy the same space and Adam could...not die. He certainly felt like he was going to. All the clichéd bodily responses you'd expect from the teenager he'd been when he'd sent Freddy away kicked in simultaneously. His heart sped up; his breath grew short; sweat collected at his hairline.

Freddy frowned at his phone "Can we try to save a chair for Ben?"

"Of course." Lulu snagged one from a neighboring table. "Is he going to meet us?"

"I'd hoped so. It's not good for him to be cooped up in that house by himself all the time. He agreed to come out, but he's backpedaling now."

Their conversation was cut short by the appearance of Lady Rusty Merlot on the tiny stage at the front of the bar. As was her custom, Lady Merlot did not greet her audience before her set; she merely launched into her first number, which tonight was the Beatles' "Drive My Car."

Freddy smiled to himself. He must have felt Adam watching him, because he looked over and met Adam's eyes. "Lady Merlot's still at it."

"She is," Adam agreed. "Some things never change."

"But some things do."

His tone was neutral, but it didn't need to be otherwise for Adam to feel the rebuke. Thankful for the dim light of the bar, he looked at the floor as his cheeks heated.

They watched the rest of the set without talking except to order a round of drinks when a server came by. When it was over, Lulu and Henry hooted and whistled. Freddy and Adam clapped less extravagantly.

"Well," Adam said, once the applause had died down, "I think I'll head—"

"Frederick Wentworth."

Damn. He'd been hoping to make an escape before Lady Merlot, who usually joined Adam for a drink between sets, appeared.

"Rusty," Freddy said, his tone completely blank, communicating nothing.

"That's Lady Merlot to you." She winked, but there was an edge to her voice as she issued the correction. "What kind of homosexual are you that you don't know that you should be using my drag name and feminine pronouns when I'm inhabiting this glorious persona?"

"I didn't know that," Henry said.

"That's because you're not a real homosexual, dear." Lady Merlot waved dismissively and didn't look at Henry as she spoke. She must have sensed that Henry was about to object, though, because then she turned and added, "You're one of those new-fangled things. Everything-sexual. Extra-sexual. Whatever."

Henry huffed a little. "Pansexual. I'd expect you to be more enlightened on the topic."

"Why? Because I'm gay? Remember, I'm also old as dirt. The most action I've gotten in the last year has been over Facebook messenger."

Adam didn't blame Henry for being a bit annoyed with Rusty. Rusty could be a giant jerk when he wanted to. And he often wanted to.

"The thing about Lady Merlot and her alter ego," Adam said, trying to smooth things over, "is that despite appearances, they're both actually pretty conservative—in the philosophical sense, I mean."

Lulu furrowed her brow. "In the what sense?"

"Like, not politically, of course, but in the sense of being resistant to change, or—"

"So what brings you back to our sleepy little hamlet, Frederick?" Lady Merlot, as was her custom when she didn't like the direction a conversation was taking, simply spoke over everyone else.

"I'm keeping Ben Captain company. He's pretty broken up about his wife."

"Ahh. Yes." Lady Merlot placed a hand to her chest. "So tragic. I always liked that Ben."

"No you didn't," Freddy said.

Lady Merlot's eyebrows shot up. She didn't like being so openly contradicted, but Freddy was correct. Rusty had always lumped Ben and Freddy in a category he used to call "the go nowheres." He'd been more concerned about Freddy than Ben, though. Ben had never posed a threat to Rusty's mission to catapult Adam out of town.

"Is Ben going to join us?" Lulu asked.

Freddy scowled at his phone. "I don't think so."

Lulu turned to Lady Merlot. "Freddy's trying to get Ben to come out of his shell a little. He's been holed up at home for so long."

"The man could do with some human connection—besides me," Freddy said. "I can't talk him into it, though."

Lady Merlot shook her head and *tsked*. "Perhaps a drag show at a crowded bar isn't the place to start."

Freddy chuckled. It looked strange on him, both objectively

and because his exchange with Lady Merlot had been, to that point, so frosty. "Point taken. But where do I start? A bush party probably isn't a great idea, either."

"Maybe you could invite a few friendly faces over to his place," Adam offered. "That might feel less overwhelming."

"Oh, that's a great idea!" Lulu said excitedly, clearly imagining herself as one of the "friendly faces" in attendance. If the town was obsessed with Freddy Wentworth as its most famous resident, his friend Ben Captain was a close second. They co-owned the Manhattan restaurant Captain's and had appeared on *Food Fanatics* together. Freddy had been the bigger personality on the show, but Ben was still famous, at least by Bishop's Glen standards. Adam knew the McGuires were dying to see Ben's house. He had a big place perched on the edge of the lake, and word was he and his wife had done major renovations when they'd bought it a few years back.

"It actually is a good idea." Freddy darted a glance at Adam.

The meager bit of praise warmed Adam's insides. Which was kind of pathetic. And enough to inspire him to push back from the table. Letting himself bask in Freddy's good opinion —even if it was only a momentary good opinion—was not wise. "I'm going to head home."

"Stay for the last set," Lady Merlot ordered.

"Sorry. I'm beat."

Lady Merlot's eyebrows rose. She was not accustomed to being openly disobeyed by Adam. As with his family, Adam usually took the path of least resistance with Rusty/Lady Merlot. *Stay for another set. Do the Toyota before the Chevy.*

Dump Freddy Wentworth.

"Did you drive?" Henry asked.

"Nope." One thing Adam did appreciate about living in

town instead of at Kellynch was that he could walk more places in less time.

Although the long walk from Kellynch to town hadn't stopped them—he sneaked a glance at Freddy—back in the day.

"If you stay, we can drive you home," Henry said.

"Thanks, but I could use the fresh air." Adam tried for polite but insistent. It was a balance he was pretty good at striking, having had a lot of practice with his family.

Everyone made their goodbyes, Freddy's version of which was merely another cool nod.

Which is why it startled the hell out of Adam when, half a block later, he heard footsteps and turned to see Freddy approaching. He let loose a breath. This wasn't the best part of town. It was too far off the beaten path for tourists, who stuck to the wineries and to the small, postcard-ified section of Main Street. So he had been prepared to defend himself if need be.

Which he would still have to do, just not in the manner he'd been thinking.

God, Freddy was still so gorgeous. As he stepped into the light cast by a streetlamp, he might as well have been an angel stepping into a sunbeam. *You look like an angel*, Adam always used to say, and Freddy would laugh and say, *You're the only one who thinks so.*

Freddy had looked like an angel, and he still did. His hair was the same messy mop of dirty blond. Adam remembered what that hair felt like, tangled up in his fingers. And those eyes, bluer than the lake on its bluest day. There were fine lines around those eyes now, but they managed to make him look even better. They conferred a gravitas that went with the brash, confident persona Adam had seen on TV. His nose, which he'd broken as a teenager, still had the telltale bump on it, but it seemed less stark on his face than it had eight years ago. Adam had always loved that bump. Somehow, the single flaw lodged in the middle of all that perfection had always made his face even more dear to Adam.

"I thought I'd head out, too."

Adam had to stifle a happy smile. He didn't flatter himself that the timing of Freddy's departure had anything to do with him, but the knowledge that Freddy wouldn't be leaving with Lulu or Henry was buoying.

"You can't be walking all the way to Ben's." The town curved around the bottom of the lake—"the Bishop's Glen Smile!" the tourism brochures proclaimed. Ben lived on the lake on other corner of the smile from where they were now.

Freddy shrugged. "We used to walk that far and farther."

It was true.

"But, no," Freddy said. He cleared his throat. His discomfort was palpable. "I, uh, thought I'd walk for a bit and then take a cab the rest of the way."

Unsure of what to say, Adam nodded. Freddy fell into step beside him, and they walked. Just liked they used to do. The slow-moving courtship of their young adulthood had started with walks—every Saturday night, after they got off their jobs at Miller's.

Those walks had been the start of everything. The best summer of Adam's life. His sexual awakening. But more than all that. It had been the start of love.

The end of it, too, it turned out.

There was more distance between them tonight—both literally and figuratively—than there used to be, but otherwise it was the same. Freddy had never seemed to mind that he had to moderate his pace to stay in step with Adam. A childhood bone infection and subsequent surgery to remove a chunk of his femur had left Adam with a permanent limp—and a fair amount of pain. As much as he liked walking, he *didn't* like doing it with other people. He always felt like he was slowing them down. But Freddy never commented on it. With Freddy, it had always felt like they were going the speed they were supposed to go. More than that, even—like their leisurely pace allowed them to notice things, to discover things, about the world and about each other. Their long, slow walks had been the mechanisms they used to reveal themselves to each other, before they discovered the vocabulary—or the guts—to speak directly about what was in their hearts.

It felt exactly the same now, though Adam understood that was an illusion. A trick of a mind that had made a mistake and bitterly regretted it. Things *weren't* the same. They couldn't go back—he'd made sure of it.

"I wanted to say..."

Freddy startled Adam out of his self-flagellation. His skin started to prickle, but he forced himself to keep walking as if he wasn't on pins and needles waiting for Freddy to finish his aborted thought. This was how big things had gotten said all those years ago. It was easier to talk while you walked.

"I didn't know it was Kellynch that Sophie was buying." Freddy blew out a breath. "I didn't put her up to it."

"I didn't think you had." He truly hadn't. Yes, he'd been knocked on his ass when he'd learned that Sophie was the purchaser, but it hadn't occurred to him to think Freddy had been pulling the strings behind the scenes. It wasn't that Adam wouldn't have deserved just that, more that he assumed Freddy was too busy with his successful life to lower himself to something as petty as revenge. Adam might not have moved on, but he had no doubt that Freddy had.

Freddy exhaled again, but this one sounded more like a sigh of relief.

"What I said before was true." Adam rushed to reassure him. "I'm glad to have someone like her at Kellynch." Adam didn't know Sophie Croft—née Wentworth—well. Freddy was two years older than Adam, and as Freddy's older sister by five years, Sophie was half a generation ahead of Adam. "I feel like she'll appreciate it, maybe more than a lot of other people would." Certainly more than his mother had.

"She will. She does."

That made Adam happy. Well, happy-sad.

"Her husband had to leave the navy because of an injury, but he still loves the water. He has a mind to start a pleasure boating business. Dinner cruises for tourists, that sort of thing."

"I imagine that will be a success. That's kind of a gap in the economy around here. The only thing close is the paddle boats and canoes you can rent downtown." It was a great idea, actually. "They could pave a little trail down to the water. Build a bigger dock."

The waterfront at Kellynch had always been utilitarian—the family had never used it for boating—but it could easily be made prettier and more accessible. Back in the day, Adam and his siblings had sometimes picked their way through the rocky shore to go swimming. Well, mostly Adam.

And Freddy. Adam and Freddy had gone swimming there quite a lot that last summer. They'd done other things in and by the water, too, scrambling up onto the dock and losing themselves in each other under cover of darkness.

He forced the memory back and made himself keep talking. "If we could get the vines back under control, we could have tastings, too. People could come early and..." No. He'd misspoken. There was no *we*. Kellynch didn't belong to the Elliots anymore.

"You," he said. "I meant you."

"Sophie," Freddy corrected, though gently. "I'm only here temporarily."

"Right."

"But it's a good idea." He paused as they approached Rook Street. "This is where you turn? You're staying at your brother's, right?"

Adam wanted to ask how Freddy knew that, but that was dumb. He was flattering himself to think Freddy had sought any special knowledge of him. This was a small, gossipy town, and probably everyone had dissected the foreclosure of Kellynch and its aftermath in minute detail. "Uh, yep, this is where I peel off."

"I'll walk you the rest of the way." Freddy gestured for Adam to make the turn ahead of him.

Adam's heart thumped. He ordered himself not to read anything into this. Freddy had always had a protective, chivalrous streak. He'd always walked Adam home back in the day, even before there was anything actually going on between them and despite the fact that it had been a ridiculously long walk to Kellynch and back to town where Freddy lived.

"I was sorry to hear about your dad," Freddy said when they'd made the turn and reestablished a rhythm.

"Thanks. It was…a shock. One day he was out there testing barrels, and the next his heart had given out."

"So you didn't get to take over like you wanted?"

Adam shook his head, embarrassed that he had ever told Freddy about that foolish dream. That he'd ever thought he was smart enough to be the winemaker at Kellynch.

"I'm sorry about that, too," said Freddy, with more gentleness than Adam deserved. "So what happened? The vineyard couldn't survive without him?"

"Pretty much. There was no succession plan in place. We had someone in to take over, but..." *Wilhelmina and Betsy spent all our operating money.* "You, ah, remember my mother?"

"Of course I do." Freddy laughed, which Adam was both surprised by and grateful for. "Do you know she cornered me that night?"

Adam didn't have to ask what night. He and Freddy had whiled away many a day—well, many a night—outside at Kellynch, or in the barrel rooms, but they'd done it alone. The one family dinner Freddy had come to had been fraught. And that hadn't even been a "I'm bringing my boyfriend to dinner" thing. Though he'd been out for a year at that point, Adam had been nervous about actually introducing Freddy as a significant other. His misgivings had been justified: when he'd announced he was bringing his friend Freddy Wentworth to dinner, his mother had started in on an interrogation about where Freddy lived and who his parents were. The phrase *town riffraff* was used more than once. Betsy had chimed in with the news that he was a high school dropout. Then Mark followed by launching a conversational grenade as he recounted Freddy's town-square sex scandal. Adam had thought maybe he could get away with the ruse that Freddy was merely a friend, but as he watched his mother's eyes narrow and her lips purse, he knew he had been naive. And though she hadn't outright forbidden him from bringing Freddy over, he'd known the dinner wouldn't go well.

But he *hadn't* known his mother actually *said* anything to Freddy that night. "She spoke to you? What did she say?" He didn't know why he was asking. He wouldn't like the answer.

"She followed me when I went to the bathroom and told

68

me outright I wasn't good enough for you." He chuckled. "I told her we were just friends."

Something in Adam rebelled, even after all these years, at the idea that Freddy had instinctively known he had to cover up the true nature of their relationship from his snobbish family.

But of course Adam had done the same thing, and done it first.

"But she wasn't having it," Freddy went on. "She said her assessment stood independent of the precise nature of our relationship."

"She *what*? Why didn't you tell me any of this?"

Freddy glanced over. "I was afraid she was onto us. I knew your relationship with your family was important to you, and that it was tenuous. But mostly I didn't tell you because I knew it would upset you, and I saw no reason to do that." He paused, then added, "At the time, I thought her opinion had no bearing on anything."

Adam wanted to explain that it hadn't. His mother never could have made him give Freddy up. Hiding who Freddy was to him, maybe. But not giving him up.

No, that distinction belonged to Rusty.

"It turns out," Freddy went on, "that her opinion was more widely held."

"Freddy, I..."

What? He what? What could he possibly say that wouldn't make him sound like Lulu McGuire, fawning all over Freddy because he'd become rich and famous? How could he explain his overreliance on Rusty's opinion back in the day? *He was there for me when no one else was? My relationship with my family was fragile, and I imagined a future in which Rusty was all I had?* It all sounded so feeble now.

Yap, yap, yap, yap, yap!

Saved by Mr. Collins.

Freddy whirled. "What the hell is that?"

Mr. Collins did have quite a unique "bark." It was like a cricket, but louder. More like a high-pitched chain saw.

The pitiful creature came loping up the street, barking his little head off. He made a beeline for Adam and started jumping up and down at his feet. When he was excited— which was a lot—Mr. Collins could jump a good two feet off the ground, which was pretty impressive considering his legs were probably only six inches long.

Freddy's laugh was a cross between delight and incredulity. "I repeat: what the hell is that?"

Adam spoke to the dog first. "Shh!" Then to Freddy: "This is Mr. Collins."

"My God. He's…"

"Ugly as sin? An assault on the eardrums? Some breeder's idea of a joke?" Adam had, despite himself, grown fond of Mr. Collins, but he held no illusions about the dog's qualities. Or lack thereof.

"What *is* he, exactly?"

"I don't know for sure. He was a stray who sort of attached himself to me. The vet's best guess is he's a greyhound-Chihuahua mix."

"Almost like one of greyhounds from the racetrack escaped and—"

"Got in on with one of Mrs. Littleton's Chihuahuas?" Mrs. Littleton owned an antique store downtown and was obsessed with her gaggle of purebred Chihuahuas, many of which she showed professionally. "Bingo."

"Wow." Freddy squatted, probably to get a better look at

Mr. Collins since the moonlight wasn't very bright. Mr. Collins *was* ugly as sin. He had huge, pointy ears that were way too big for his head, bulging milky-blue eyes, and a scrawny body encased in a layer of fur so thin he looked bald from afar.

Mr. Collins started wagging his tail and licking Freddy's face. Mr. Collins was ugly, but he gave his affections easily, and once given, they remained fixed.

"What do you mean he attached himself to you?"

"He just kept coming around. Would never leave no matter what I did or said. It was like he wouldn't take no for an answer. I'd yell at him to go away, but he'd just lick me." Which sounded stupid when he explained it like that. Mr. Collins was a dog. What did it say about Adam that he'd let himself be outmaneuvered by a dog, and one of Mr. Collin's small stature and low intelligence at that?

Probably the same thing it said about him that he'd let Rusty convince him to give up the love of his life.

They'd arrived at Mark's. "Well, this is me. It was, uh…" What? What could he possibly say? *Nice to see you? Alarming to see you?*

Gutting to see you?

Freddy just nodded. "I'll wait until you get inside."

That was so Freddy-like. "I'm actually around back. In an RV." He lifted his chin as he spoke. He was used to people looking down on the fact that he lived in an RV. But he didn't care—or at least he didn't care enough to change anything. That sucker was paid for, and more important, it was *home*. The home he'd finally made for himself, independent of his family.

Freddy raised his eyebrows, not in disapproval so much, Adam thought, as surprise. He gestured toward the backyard.

He wasn't going to leave until he'd seen Adam safely to his door.

"Well," Freddy said when they'd tromped around back. "Look at this."

"I moved out of the house at Kellynch shortly after my dad died," Adam said, answering the unasked question. "I drove this here after, uh, Sophie bought the place. Gotta figure out what's next. Probably I should just get a lot in a park, but…"

"You can't stand the idea of living cheek-by-jowl with other people. You'd be better off buying a chunk of forest and parking it there."

Freddy still knew him. It was unnerving.

Adam had picked up Mr. Collins, and now he stooped to let him down. He pointed at the RV. "Go inside."

The dog obeyed, disappearing through the doggie door Adam had built him.

Freddy laughed. "He has his own little door."

"Yeah. I work long days sometimes, so he needs to be able to get out. But honestly, one of these days the dumb mutt is going to meet his doom. It's not so bad here, but there were coyotes in the woods near Kellynch."

Freddy nodded but didn't say anything.

What happened now? Should he invite Freddy in?

"Well, I'll be off," Freddy said.

Apparently not.

"I shouldn't have left Ben this long. He's…" Freddy looked at the sky and sighed.

"You want me to run you home?" Adam asked.

That drew Freddy's attention. He chuckled. "In this thing?"

Adam smiled. "I have a car."

"You just prefer walking."

Yep, Freddy still knew him. "I do."

"I do, too."

And with that, Freddy gave Adam another of those inscrutable nods, turned on his heel, and disappeared into the night.

CHAPTER SIX

Eight years ago

"There's nothing wrong with your car. The cable to the battery is just...not connected." Adam emerged from under the hood of Freddy's Mustang wearing a quizzical look.

Shit. Was he busted? Freddy's car, as much of a piece of junk as it was, was fine. He'd left it at home last Saturday night so he'd have an excuse to walk with Adam. And then the invitation to bring it by Anderson Motors had been too much to pass up. So, yes, he'd googled, *how to make a car not start*, disconnected his own goddamn battery, and *paid for a tow* to Anderson Motors.

But, oh, it had been worth it. Adam was so adorable in his mechanic persona. Instead of the coveralls Freddy would have expected, Adam wore black cargo pants and a tight, grease-spattered, red T-shirt. He also had grease on his forearms, and a little bit on one cheek. Freddy's hands twitched. They wanted to touch that cheek, to wipe that stain off and maybe linger long enough to—

"You figure it out?" Rusty Anderson emerged from the office.

"Yep," Adam said. "Just a loose battery cable. Easy as pie."

If Adam had looked quizzical after he'd discovered the problem, Rusty did not. He went straight for *suspicious as hell*. Well, they couldn't prove anything.

Freddy schooled his expression to neutrality and got out his wallet. "How much do I owe you?"

"Oh, nothing." Adam held up his palms. "It took me two seconds."

"Still, you have to let me pay you."

"No," Adam said. "I insist."

"Well, okay, thanks. But at least let me buy you a coffee or something. I was going to pop over to the bakery for coffee and a bagel anyway."

Please say yes.

Adam blushed and looked at the ground. It was so, so satisfying to see him blush in the bright light of day. His pale skin, which was actually smattered with a few unlikely, faint freckles, went pink all at once. There was no slow spread of color, just an immediate saturation. It did something to Freddy's dick, which was one thing, but it *also* did something to his chest, and that thing was less familiar. Unsettling. But addictive.

Please say yes.

"Okay, thanks. I'm, uh, due for a break anyway."

Adam glanced at Rusty, and Freddy's gaze followed. Rusty was Adam's boss, of course, and the way Adam talked about him, it seemed like Rusty had a lot of influence over Adam. But Freddy had a hard time imagining the workplace culture at Anderson Motors was such that Adam had to ask if he could take a break.

But something was up Rusty's butt. He pressed his lips into a thin line, and his gaze flickered between Adam and Freddy. Finally he said, with practically no inflection in his tone, "Bring me a cappuccino," and turned back to the office.

Present day

"It's just dinner."

"I know. I just don't understand why you had to spring this on me with no warning."

Freddy pressed his fingers against his temples. He tried to remind himself that there was no template for grieving. That Ben had loved his wife with a fierceness that Freddy had never felt... Well, that he hadn't felt for quite some time. "I just think some human company would do you good."

"You're here."

"For now." He left unsaid that eventually, one or both of them would have to return to Captain's. They were its executive chefs, which meant they weren't necessarily needed for its day-to-day operations, but they did have their names attached to the place. Reputation mattered. And they'd never been away this long, even when they'd been filming *Food Fanatics*. He was relying on the fact that Sherry, their head chef, could be trusted absolutely, but soon the restaurant would have to turn over the menu for fall, and Freddy or Ben would be needed.

"You want to go back, go back," Ben said. "You don't need to babysit me."

"I don't want to go back."

Freddy was surprised by how true it was. He thought he'd

come here reluctantly—and he had—but it was surprisingly nice being out of the city. Not in Bishop's Glen particularly, but back somewhere he could breathe in that green smell. See the stars he'd forgotten were up there.

Freddy had taken Adam's suggestion to heart and decided that if he couldn't coax Ben out into the world, he would bring a little of the world to Ben. He *had* sort of sprung it on Ben at the last minute—it was two o'clock, and the McGuires were due at seven—but that was by design. Less time for Ben to freak out.

"I thought I'd do ravioli," Freddy said. Ravioli was a calculated manipulation. It was Ben's signature dish, and he always maintained that Freddy's wasn't up to par. "I got some squash at the farmer's market this morning."

"You suck at pasta."

Freddy performed a shrug. "Well, I already have the squash, and I also picked up some decent-tasting local ricotta, so it's getting made one way or another."

"It would be better with goat cheese," Ben said. "Ricotta, even good ricotta, is boring."

Freddy just raised his eyebrows and tried not to grin. He'd won.

"Damn you." Ben shook his head. "Who's coming?"

"Henry and Lulu McGuire."

"That's it?"

They were really the only people he'd become reacquainted with since he'd been back. Also, he pretty much hated everyone in this town, and, back in the day at least, the feeling had been mutual. Anyway, he hadn't wanted to overwhelm Ben with huge numbers. "That's it. Did you know Henry swings both ways now—all ways, actually?"

"I barely remember him."

"Well, he didn't used to."

Ben smirked. It was nice to see, so Freddy played it up by waggling his eyebrows.

"All right, go for it. But invite some more people."

"Really?" That was the last thing he'd expected from Ben.

"Yeah. If you're into Henry, we need more people. It's going to be weird and double-date-like otherwise, and I'm not—"

His voice cracked, and Freddy felt like a dick. He wasn't into Henry, not really. He might be good for a little fun if the opportunity presented itself, but that was it. Freddy hadn't been thinking about the dynamic of the dinner. Realistically, both Henry and Lulu would be flirting with him, which would leave Ben out of things—which missed the point of the exercise entirely.

"Of course." He laid a hand on his friend's shoulder. "I'll rustle up some more guests."

Hey. This is Freddy. Lulu gave me your number. What are you doing tonight?

Adam let his phone clatter onto the hood of the Corolla he'd just finished with.

What he was doing tonight was working on an emergency repair for Mrs. Littleton—she of Chihuahua fame—and then he was planning to go to career night at the high school and man the Anderson Motors booth because Rusty had decided to set up a "How to Become a Drag Queen in Five Easy Steps" booth, and Adam was afraid the Anderson booth would be neglected.

The irony wasn't lost on him. Rusty, who'd spent years nagging Adam to get out of town and go to college, now needed him to explain to teenagers why they should consider fixing cars for a living.

He picked up his phone to type a reply.

Nothing.

Freddy: Can you come to dinner at Ben's around seven? I took your advice, and I'm having some people over for dinner.

The idea that Freddy would want him to come. That after all that had come between them, he would still seek Adam out... Butterflies marshaled in his stomach.

Adam: Sure. What can I bring?

Freddy: People. Ben, uncharacteristically, wants a crowd. I don't really know anyone in this town anymore. Can you bring your brother and sister-in-law, maybe? Or anyone, really.

So much for feeling special that Freddy had chosen him. But watch how fast Adam could set aside his pride. He'd had too much of it, by proxy, back in the day, and tonight he was going to listen to the part of him that just wanted to be with Freddy, at any cost, under any circumstances, even those in which he was merely a seat-warmer.

Adam: You got it. See you soon.

CHAPTER SEVEN

Eight years ago

When Freddy had considered love, which wasn't often, he'd assumed it would be messy. In movies, there was always some big misunderstanding that drove the lovers apart. There was plotting, angst, suffering. No thanks. It all seemed way too exhausting.

It turned out falling in love was the easiest thing in the world. All he had to do was walk.

And with each step, he fell a little more.

"You don't have to keep walking me, you know," Adam said shyly. They were twenty minutes into what had become their regular Saturday night walk out to Kellynch. Adam usually said some variation on this, but he always waited until they were well underway, which suggested to Freddy that he didn't really mean it.

Freddy made a vaguely dismissive noise. He used to say things like *You're on to something with all this walking. It does clear the head.* But they were beyond that now. Now, it was enough to dismiss the sentiment and let Adam fill in the rest. Which was that he wanted to be here. Didn't care that it would be four in the morning by the time he finally got home, having trekked a total of eleven miles.

Which wasn't to say it was all easy logistically. It was easy emotionally, but sometimes he didn't know what to *do*. Whether, for example, it would be okay to grab Adam's hand at some point.

God. Listen to him. Freddy used to be a certified slut. After the unfortunate town-square dick-sucking debacle, he'd made a rule not to hook up with people in Bishop's Glen proper, but the region was full of towns—and tourists. He got laid a lot. Well, he used to. And he had *never* gotten himself twisted into knots over *holding hands*, for fuck's sake.

But it wasn't like he'd gone all heart-eyed-emoji soft. Well, he had, but he was still *himself*. He didn't want to *just* hold hands with Adam. He wanted to kiss him. All over. He wanted to strip him bare and look at every inch of his pale skin. He wanted to fuck him. And it was always there, that desire. It was just that he didn't know how, or whether, to act on it. When it wasn't just a hookup, this shit mattered. You had to do things at the right pace. In the right order.

Because the thing was, he'd *told* Adam stuff. About how he stupidly, irrationally, wanted to know his dad. Or at least know *about* him. But that he was too proud to ask his mother for details—because she was proud, too.

About how he'd dropped out of school because he didn't realistically see himself doing anything that required the diploma, so why go and subject himself to all the shit everyone gave him every day when he could be out making money?

Confidences had been exchanged, was the point. And

whether Adam knew it or not—whether he wanted it or not—he had Freddy's heart. Freddy might have a lot of sexual experience, but he had no experience with love. So, as easy as it had been to fall, it made things weird sometimes.

One of the awkward logistical spots was always the foot of the driveway to Kellynch, where they parted ways. He never knew how to extricate himself—probably because he didn't *want* to extricate himself. Usually they talked for a few minutes, Freddy kicking the gravel like he was an aw-shucks character out of Mayberry, searching for something to say to extend his stay—something dumb like asking Adam about the flowers on the property. Eventually, Freddy would turn around and start the long walk home.

Tonight had started the same as always, with Adam saying, "Thanks for keeping me company."

"No problem." Freddy had just started doing his gravel kicking thing when, holy fuck, *Adam* kissed *him*.

He was so startled that he jerked his head a little, so Adam's mouth landed on his jaw instead of his lips. Adam started to pull away, but Freddy shot his hand out, grabbed the back of Adam's head, and corrected his aim. Brought their foreheads together.

And *Jesus Christ*. If Freddy had known that actually having your heart invested in someone could make touching them feel like this, maybe he would have tried to fall in love sooner. Because as they stayed there, their lips almost but not quite touching, fireworks went off inside Freddy. He was breathing as hard suddenly as if he had run all the way from town.

He wasn't sure who moved, just that what had been half an inch of space between them became none. Adam's lips were so impossibly soft that Freddy couldn't stifle a groan. His jaw went slack with desire, and this brought Adam's tongue in contact with his mouth, and he was sure he would die because—

"Eww."

—because Adam was pulling away?

He'd been about to expire from the pure, undiluted pleasure of Adam's tongue in his mouth, but it turned out that *not* having Adam's tongue in his mouth was way, way more dangerous.

But, okay, he needed to tune into what was happening here because if he'd done anything to push Adam, to make him feel unsafe, he'd just walk into the woods right now and kill himself.

But no. Adam was grinning. Kind of sheepishly, but still, he didn't look upset.

"I don't kiss smokers," he said.

Freddy laughed. You had to admire the guy. He'd been expecting to be rebuffed with any number of objections, the most likely of which would have been some variation on *You're not good enough for me.* Adam wouldn't have said it like that, of course. He was too good-hearted. But Freddy would have known how to interpret *I think we should just be friends* or *I'm not really looking for a boyfriend right now.* He knew what everyone thought of him.

"Right," he said, unable to resist returning the grin Adam was still sporting. "I guess I should be going anyway." Adam nodded, and Freddy turned and started the long trudge home.

Once Kellynch was out of sight, he lit a cigarette and told himself to enjoy it, because it would be the last one he ever smoked.

Present day

Five hours after Freddy's text, instead of trying to bring Mrs. Littleton's Buick back from the dead, Adam found himself climbing the steps to Ben Captain's lake place.

"Oh, my God, I've always wanted to see this place!" Chloe was practically levitating with glee. When Adam had told Mark and Chloe about the invitation and suggested that one of them come with him, suddenly they'd been able to find childcare that wasn't him. He'd thought about inviting Rusty, who, like Chloe, had been intensely curious-bordering-on-nosy about Ben and Ben's house—so much so that he probably would've happily thrown over career night, but Adam had decided that would be a mistake. That night at Whine, Rusty and Freddy had been...well, not cold toward each other exactly, but not overjoyed to see each other. Freddy had never seemed to be a fan of Rusty. And Rusty, of course, felt the same way. If Adam invited him along, he would come, but then Adam would be all paranoid about his behavior, worried that Rusty would accuse him later of falling for Freddy again.

And he would be right. Except not again. There was no *again*. There was only *still. Always.*

"Hey." Freddy opened Ben's front door before they could knock, and Adam's stomach did a funny little dance. Freddy's glance slid over everyone, and Adam thought for a moment it might have lingered a beat longer on him than on the others but decided no, he'd been imagining that. "Thanks for coming."

"Thanks for having us," Adam said, as Chloe and Mark pushed their way inside. He handed Freddy a bouquet of peonies, which used to be his favorite. Even if Freddy hadn't let his gaze linger on Adam just now, Adam was pretty sure he wasn't imagining the extra-long look Freddy gave the flowers.

Freddy had admired the peonies at the bottom of the driveway at Kellynch, and Adam had decided one night—the night they tried to kiss for the first time—to give him one on the next visit. That had started a tradition of Adam cutting Freddy a blossom each Saturday night before they parted ways. He still remembered Freddy's shock the first time he'd done it. "Nobody's ever given me anything like this," he'd said —and then he'd grinned and kissed Adam so hard he'd almost seen stars.

Peonies grew all over Kellynch this time of year.

But Adam, seeing as he was no longer Adam Elliot of Kellynch Estates, had had to buy the flowers at a florist.

Inside, the McGuire siblings were already sipping wine. Ben was introduced, though in a town like Bishop's Glen, everyone generally knew each other by sight or by family connection if not firsthand.

"I used to work at Greta's Grocery, so I knew your father a little," Mark said to Ben. "He was a regular customer."

"I hope you won't hold that against me." Ben smiled to indicate he was teasing. Ben's father had worked at a popsicle factory that closed when Adam was a kid. The workers had been laid off, but Ben's dad had never really found his feet again and he'd become quite a conspicuous alcoholic. He often appeared in the crime blotter Wilhelmina and Betsy liked to read.

No one here would hold that against Ben, though. *Rusty* would have, which ratified Adam's decision not to bring him along. "The go-nowheres": Ben was, unbeknownst to himself, a founding member.

"And I'm older than you all." Sophie greeted them with a

smile. "So I'm not sure we've ever met formally. This is my husband, Geordie."

Adam froze for a moment. He hadn't realized Sophie would be here. But that was stupid. Freddy had been desperate for guests—that was the only reason Adam himself was here—so of course he would invite his sister and her husband.

He was still stuck, unsure what do to as he stood near the kitchen island while everyone else fanned out into the main living space, when Sophie came over and laid a hand on his arm.

Her nails were shaped exactly like Freddy's, Adam realized with a jolt.

"I want you to know I'm sorry your family lost Kellynch and also that I plan to take very good care of it." She spoke softly, so that only he could hear, and with such seemingly genuine kindness that some of his unease dissipated.

"Thank you," he managed. "It's a special place."

"This house is *gorgeous*," Chloe cried, drawing their attention. Adam was torn between relief at being interrupted and embarrassment as her eyes bugged out as she took in the home's interior. Adam tried not to be flustered by his family's naked ambition, but they sure made it difficult sometimes.

The reno really had been stunning, though—he was just better at controlling his eyeballs than Chloe was hers. The original log cabin structure had been expanded on and the interior walls torn down to create a great room where the kitchen bled seamlessly into dining and living spaces. The log walls and rustic wooden planked floors gave everything a warm, homey feel. Although the space had been made bigger and more functional, it retained its original character. Adam appreciated that.

Soon, everyone was sitting in the living area except Freddy, who was cooking, and Ben, who was sitting on a stool at his kitchen island halfway between Freddy and the others, bossing Freddy around.

"Go away!" Freddy finally said. "You're cramping my style."

"That's because you suck at pasta." Ben smirked. If he was really as distraught as Freddy had suggested, it was good to see him in a teasing mood.

Freddy took a sip of his wine with one hand and pointed toward the living room with the other. "I love you, man, but go."

"You were a lot meaner on TV," Chloe said, and everyone laughed.

"That's true!" Sophie said. "TV Freddy never would have admitted to loving anyone."

Ben came to sit on the sofa. "They kind of created a persona for him that was a lot meaner than he actually is."

"I am, too, mean!" Freddy called from the kitchen.

"He's a big softie," Ben stage-whispered. Then he raised his voice. "Who can't make pasta to save his life."

Adam could see the McGuires and Mark and Chloe struggling to absorb the idea that Freddy was, to quote Ben, a big softie. To be fair, that wasn't a side of Freddy anyone had really seen, back in the day. Anyone else. Adam had seen it.

"How hard is pasta?" Chloe asked.

"I think it's homemade pasta," Adam said. He'd seen Freddy rolling out big sheets of dough and cutting little squares out of them.

"Wow." Lulu popped up and made her way over to the kitchen. "I need to see this."

Adam noticed that Freddy didn't object to Lulu's help the

way he had Ben's. In fact, he started showing her how to seal the edges of the raviolis. The rest of them continued chatting, but Adam couldn't prevent himself from straining to overhear what was happening in the kitchen. They seemed to have moved on to making an avocado salad.

"Give them a squeeze to see if they're ripe," Freddy was saying. "There's nothing worse than a woody avocado."

"How's this?" Lulu asked.

Freddy's fingers closed around the fruit. "That one's too hard."

"I don't know. I enjoy squeezing hard things."

Freddy laughed, and Adam's face flamed as if he were the target of Lulu's double entendre.

And he was so jealous. *God*, he was jealous. If he'd done things differently eight years ago, it might have been him there in the kitchen, helping Freddy. Bantering with him. Instead, his life was the same as it had always been. He fixed cars, he read books, he played with his niece and nephew, he went to Whine on Saturday nights. It wasn't that he didn't like those things or that he yearned for a bigger life. As he always told Rusty when he was on one of his rants about how Adam should leave town, he *liked* Bishop's Glen. He had no ambition to live anywhere else. It was just that seeing Freddy again had thrown into sharp relief how...heartbroken he still was. How much cutting Freddy out of his life had been like cutting off a limb. And since he'd just been thinking that losing Kellynch was like losing a limb, he didn't have too many of those left.

A bit overcome, Adam got up and walked to the other side of the room under the guise of looking out the sliding glass doors to the deck and the lake beyond. It was better to take himself out of listening range of the kitchen. He let the swirls of conversation from the living room wash over him without really hearing anything.

Eight years had gone by. He should be over this.

Adam, in an attempt to become a proper gay, had hooked up with a few guys in those eight years—well, four, to be precise, and they'd all been in the first two years.

Which was totally pathetic when he thought about it. Part of him had hoped that one of those hookups might lead to more. To an actual relationship. And to be fair, one or two of the guys might have been game. It was just that no one had ever measured up to Freddy. When you fell madly in love with the first person you ever had sex with, it was hard to settle for just sex. He'd tried. It had been easy enough to find guys to have sex with—to exchange physical touch with until they both got off. What he couldn't replace was *Freddy*. The way Freddy had cared about him. Walked everywhere with him. Patiently taught him what his body, which had always been something of a millstone to Adam, was capable of. Acted like the clumsy blow jobs Adam gave him on the dock were the greatest thing ever. And then blown Adam's mind in return.

It was just...never like that again.

Eventually, he'd decided that hookups weren't worth it. His own hand was less trouble.

The worst part was that Freddy was clearly not so affected. Though he was older than Adam, he seemed younger at heart. He wasn't wearing heartbreak like a heavy yoke the way Adam was. He'd bounced back.

Of course he'd bounced back. He'd gone on to be wildly successful and had men and women alike throwing them-selves at him. While Adam's life had stayed exactly the same, Freddy's had expanded.

Lost in his thoughts, he wasn't aware of how much time

had passed until he felt someone approach. It was Freddy, carrying one of the stools from the kitchen island. Without a word, he set it down next to Adam. He didn't smile or nod or do anything, just deposited the stool and made his way back to the kitchen.

Adam's leg *was* hurting. Damn Freddy. Did he have to be so observant and thoughtful all the time? He never could stand to see Adam suffering. Or, forget suffering—he could never stand to see Adam ever-so-slightly inconvenienced. And apparently even the passing of eight years—even betrayal— could not temper his reflexive kindness. Adam felt again what he had lost when he'd forsaken Freddy.

At dinner, Adam was seated next to Ben, who surprised him by being an avid reader. That certainly hadn't come out on *Food Fanatics*.

"I've been reading Thomas Hardy lately," Ben said. "Somehow I never got to him. I just finished *Tess of the D'Urbervilles*."

"Well, that can't be good for you right now," Adam said, and instantly regretted it. Who was he to tell a grieving man what to read? He tried to make a joke. "I mean, sexual assault, suicide." He thought back to the book. "Turnips. So many turnips."

"She does pull a lot of turnips, doesn't she?" Ben laughed. "You sound like Freddy. I think he thinks I'm wallowing unnecessarily. Maybe I am. I've been taking a certain macabre comfort in reading this depressing stuff, but maybe I need to branch out. What would you prescribe?"

Adam gave it some thought. "A romance novel, maybe?"

Ben laughed. "Can't say I've ever tried one, but if someone of your taste is recommending them, I'll give it a shot. Give me a title."

"Well, I mostly read queer ones." Adam tried to backpedal. What had he been thinking recommending romance novels to this straight man he hardly knew? Who, even worse, was Freddy's best friend?

"Even better," Ben proclaimed, "if your aim is to get me out of my own head and life. Give me a title and I'll read it, but only if you promise to make yourself available for discussion when I'm done."

Adam was happy to agree. He never talked about books with anyone. His family was certainly not going to fit that bill, and Rusty favored mysteries, which had never been Adam's thing.

Before he knew it, dessert was being served. He and Ben had been yakking happily without noticing the passage of time. As a platter of individual apple turnovers being passed around reached him, he looked up to find Freddy staring at him from across the table. His eyes moved to Ben and then back to Adam. Suddenly, he smiled—Adam thought so, anyway. No sooner had he flashed a smile than he'd pressed his lips together to extinguish it and turned his head to obscure his face. It was like he'd been overcome for a moment with a goodwill he did not want Adam to witness—like watching the sun peek out for just a moment from behind fast-moving clouds and then be subsumed again.

But Adam had seen that secret smile just the same, and it might as well have been a knife to the gut because it reminded him so sharply, so exquisitely, of what he had lost.

CHAPTER EIGHT

Eight years ago

I don't kiss smokers.

A week had gone by since he'd dropped that little nugget, and Adam was still embarrassed.

I don't kiss smokers. Like, what? He had a *policy* or something?

He didn't kiss *anybody*. Not only was he a nineteen-year-old virgin, he had literally never been kissed.

Unless you counted the mis-aimed and then aborted attempt of last week.

God, he wished he could take it back. It wasn't that big of a deal. Certainly not if it meant he got to *kiss Freddy Wentworth.*

He'd just been so surprised by the ashtray taste. Being with Freddy, thinking about Freddy—these caused certain associations in his mind. Freddy was sweet and funny and kind. Even though they only ever saw each other at night—except that one time Freddy came to the garage and they went for coffee—he associated Freddy with lightness. In every sense of the word. Freddy made him feel like his body required less effort than usual to be in the world. He made him feel like he could see into previously shadowed places—including his heart—clearly.

So when he'd finally gotten up the nerve to make a move—and Freddy, in his usual Freddy way, had come to his assistance when it seemed like he was going to botch it—the taste of him had been a shock. Ashy and acidic and just...gross.

But not gross enough to stop kissing him, for God's sake. The pullback had been instinctive—and regretted.

Anyway, he'd decided to try to right the ship tonight. They were in the middle of a heatwave, and even though it was after midnight, it was still quite hot. Freddy had been sweating heavily when they'd set out from Miller's. Adam, as a valet, got to work outside. He could only imagine how hot the kitchen must be.

So when they reached the edge of the drive, where things usually got a little weird, his whole body practically vibrated with anxiety. He tried to preempt the usual awkwardness that descended here by reciting the three sentences he'd been practicing in his head for the last hour: "It's so hot. I'm going to go for a swim in the lake. Do you want to join me?"

"Yeah," Freddy said. "That would be great."

Well, that had been easy. Like pretty much everything with Freddy, actually. Adam often felt awkward in social situations, but, bottom-of-the-drive goodbyes aside, not with Freddy. Soon, they were on their way to the water. Kellynch gradually sloped down to a rocky shore. Adam pulled his shirt off as they walked, but said, "I recommend keeping your shoes on until you get onto the dock."

He could hear Freddy removing his shirt, and *whoa*. The idea that he could just turn around, and there would be Freddy Wentworth, shirtless. Freddy was broad chested. Adam wasn't sure if that was just the way he was built, or if it was the result of a concerted effort. In all their rambling conversations, Freddy had referenced a home gym he'd assembled in his mother's basement, so Adam assumed the latter.

He kept going without turning, wanting to prolong the reward, like a kid saving his last piece of Halloween candy.

There was a shed right at the edge of the water, and Adam opened it to retrieve a flashlight—both because it was dark and Freddy wouldn't know the dock by feel like Adam did, and because, well…eventually he was going to eat that piece of Halloween candy, and he wanted to be able to *see*.

It was an upright, lantern-style flashlight. He turned it on, walked to the end of the dock, and set it down. Then he sat and started taking his shoes off. He felt Freddy sinking down next to him. Heard the swish of his Docs being unlaced.

Finally, finally, when he couldn't stand it anymore, he turned and looked.

And *oh, my*.

Yep, the source of Freddy's bulk was definitely that home gym. He wasn't like the Incredible Hulk, but each muscle in his arms, shoulders, and chest was defined. And he had a tattoo—of course he did. Some kind of Celtic-looking design snaked around one bicep.

Adam might be bookish, but he wasn't immune to such a display of fleshly beauty. It was too much, almost. He had to look away.

But just as he was about to, something caught his eye. A big Band-Aid on Freddy's arm, just above the tattoo.

"Did you hurt yourself?" Before he could think better of it, Adam reached out and brushed his fingers over the Band-Aid.

What was he doing? He started to pull away, but Freddy reached around with his other hand and covered Adam's, effectively keeping his fingers where they were.

"Nope. That's a nicotine patch."

Present day

After dinner, Ben took Adam down to the lake. Freddy might have been jealous were he not supremely confident in Ben's unambiguous heterosexuality. Instead, he was once again overcome with a rush of gratitude and goodwill toward Adam for being the one thing in the time since Ben's wife had died that had drawn Ben out of his grief.

The two of them were remarkably similar, now that he thought about it. They were both contemplative sorts more at home with their heads in a book than in the real world. Yet they could both become animated and downright charming given the right inducement.

Where they diverged was physically. Ben, tall and conventionally handsome, looked like a movie star, which was part of why the *Food Fanatics* team had decided to position him as the "good guy" chef on the show. Adam, who was only five-seven, had an unusual collection of features: a fine, small nose, a smattering of freckles that had always seemed out of sync with his dark hair, and dark brown irises that were almost indistinguishable from his pupils.

And yet, to Freddy, Adam was sexier—by several orders of magnitude.

Some of that was probably down to the fact that Ben was Freddy's longtime, decidedly straight, platonic friend. Freddy had never thought of him as anything else and never would.

But some of it was just...Adam. The sight of him, standing at the valet stand at Miller's Inn, had always set Freddy's pulse pounding. And then, later, being able to examine those freckles—and the ones on his body—up close? It had nearly undone Freddy.

He still wasn't over it.

"Oh, Freddy, let's go down to the lake now!" Lulu cried as they finished with the dishes.

He sighed. Lulu was wearing thin. She was nice enough, but her striving was so plain, it was impossible to find her attractive. And yet, she could serve a purpose. Namely, reminding him to hang on to his pride. In this damn town, it was all he had.

"All right." He dried his hands on a towel. He'd deflected her previous suggestion that they walk to the lake, wanting to give Adam and Ben space to continue their chat unmolested. But what the hell? It was a beautiful night, and a walk in the real world was certainly preferable to the agonized strolling down memory lane he'd been doing. He looked at Henry, who'd been wiping the table. "Will you join us?" Henry happily agreed as Lulu pouted. Given a choice, Freddy would have preferred the attentions of Henry, but word was that Henry was on again with his sometime girlfriend Charlotte Haywick.

"Let's all go," Freddy said, gesturing for everyone else to join them, too. The bigger the crowd, the more buffer there would be between Lulu and him. Mark and Chloe easily agreed, as did Sophie and Geordie after a bit of coaxing— they'd been snuggled up on the sofa together. The bigger the group got, the more Lulu's pout seemed to deepen. Freddy tried not to find it funny. Maybe he *should* talk himself into the idea of a fling with Lulu. God knew, he could use the distraction.

It was nearing the end of June, so twilight was just descending even though it was late. Freddy led the way down the terraced yard to the lake. Ben really did have a beautiful place here. The house was high on a cliff, and whereas most people on this stretch of waterfront built steep staircases down to the lake, Ben had had chunks of garden and yard carved out of the cliff, creating the appearance of levels or stories. A path ran through these terraces, functioning as a switchback as it wound through the steep yard until it reached the beach and dock at water level.

"Oh, this is fun!" Lulu said, jumping from one level of yard to the next instead of following the path like everyone else.

"Careful!" Freddy called, drawing the attention of Ben and Adam.

The sight of Adam looking at him from below, his eyes wide, sent a sudden jolt down Freddy's spine. That was exactly what he used to look like when he sucked Freddy's dick. Like what was happening was the most amazing thing he'd ever been part of.

Lulu heaved a theatrical sigh, stealing his attention from Adam. See? Lulu did have diversionary potential. She put her hands on her hips, a parody of martyrdom. But she had paused in her descent and was waiting for them to catch up. "You just don't want me to have any fun, do you, Freddy?"

"Yes," he deadpanned as the larger group arrived on her level, which was one above the beach. "My sole aim in life is to curtail your fun, Lulu." He shot her a wink.

She didn't say anything, didn't even move as the rest of them continued past her. It was only when they'd arrived at the beach and were standing below her that she cried, "Catch me, Freddy!"

And God help him, she jumped. What could he do but play the role she'd forced him into? He lunged and caught her, swallowing a cry of pain as her landing felt like it nearly tore his arms out of their sockets.

"Eee!" She wrapped her arms around his neck. "That was fun!" He got the distinct sense that she wanted him to do something silly like twirl her around.

That was not happening. Irritated by her little stunt, he set her on her feet. She did not let go of his neck. He was forced to shake his head and step back rather forcefully to get her to let go of him.

"Lulu!" Henry scolded. "That could have been a disaster."

Lulu harrumphed. "Oh, it was fine. Freddy will always save me, won't you?"

Freddy's silence must have been taken as assent, for she skipped off down the dock.

The others gathered on the beach. The first stars were coming out, and as if by silent agreement, they all tilted their heads back to look at them. The sky, midnight blue, hovered on the tipping point between twilight and true night. God, the *colors* here. He'd forgotten about them, apparently, too busy with his nose to the gray grindstone in New York.

"I think I see a fish!" Lulu called from the dock. "Freddy, come see!"

He was about to reply that certainly it was too dark to see a fish—the lake was murky even under the sun of high noon—when she jumped in.

Or fell? She must have fallen. People didn't just jump fully clothed into lakes during dinner parties.

Yes, she must have fallen, judging by her brother's alarmed shout. Actually, everyone was shouting all of a sudden. He recognized his sister's shriek.

Shit. Freddy's annoyance at Lulu, who was splashing and sputtering in the water—surely she could swim, right?—was replaced by fear. It was hard to believe a person could grow up in a lake town and not know how to swim, but she wasn't doing a very good job keeping herself afloat as she thrashed.

"The lake is deep here!" Ben voice was laced with panic.

Chloe and Mark both started waving their hands and yelling and generally being unhelpful. His sister was patting her pockets, looking for her phone. "Geordie! Where's my purse? Did I leave it in the car?" Her voice was high, as it always was when she was upset.

Freddy tried to get past everyone, to join Ben, who'd run down the dock. They had to do something. But what? He looked around in vain for a life preserver.

And then Adam jumped in the lake.

Adam was a strong swimmer. The two of them had passed many a moonlit night in the water at Kellynch. Warmth spread through him at the memory of Adam's smooth, lean chest painted with silver moonlight. Of Adam laughing and splashing him. Confessing that he loved to swim because his leg wasn't such a hindrance in the water.

Of Adam gasping, even as he turned Freddy inside out.

But he had to get ahold of himself. Now was not the time for lust-tinged nostalgia.

Adam had Lulu in one arm and was using the other to swim them both to safety. Ben was kneeling on the dock, and Freddy joined him, preparing to help.

"She's bleeding—I think from the head. She must have hit it on the dock as she went in." Adam's voice was calm and strong as he and his cargo arrived dockside. As Ben grabbed Lulu under her arms to hoist her up, Adam said, "Henry, call 911. She's probably fine, but we should make sure the wound isn't too deep. After you've called, walk out to the main road to meet them." Then, still in the water, he turned his attention to Freddy. "Can you go upstairs and find flashlights and blankets? We'll need to keep her warm so she doesn't go into shock."

"Adam! Adam! What can I do?" Chloe called. Freddy sensed rather than saw Adam roll his eyes.

"You can help me, Chloe," Freddy said, knowing that the best thing to do was to get her out of the way.

"Thank you," Adam whispered.

Freddy was seized with a strong desire to help Adam out of the water, but he'd received his instructions, and Adam was perfectly capable of managing on his own, so he took Chloe's arm and ran for the house.

On his way back with an armful of towels and blankets, Chloe lighting the way with a pair of flashlights, he couldn't help but think about how impressive Adam had been just then. The way he'd calmly taken over, not just saving Lulu but authoritatively dispensing tasks to the others, making a decisive judgment call about what sort of action was needed. Adam had always been quietly capable, taking care of things for his family behind the scenes, not allowing their drama to infect him. It seemed he still possessed that same understated competence.

Understated competence should not be such a turn-on.

Freddy shook his head and reminded himself *again* that now was not the time.

Not that there ever would be a time. *Pride. Have some goddamn pride.*

Adam had been quite clear about not wanting Freddy, in the end, and Freddy would not lower himself to suggest that decision be revisited.

CHAPTER NINE

Eight years ago

"Hi."

How was it possible that one syllable was capable of turning Freddy's insides to mush? It had been an extra-busy shift at Miller's, and meeting up with Adam afterward was like sinking into a warm, comforting bath. Or maybe a warm, comforting bath into which someone had dropped a hair dryer, because with Adam, the warmth of familiarity co-existed with an electric current of lust. The way Adam had been so clearly waiting for him. The way his eyes had lit up and he'd flashed Freddy a quick, quiet smile. The way he'd reached out and quickly laid his hand against Freddy's face in a gesture that was both a tender greeting and an exhilarating expression of possession. It was swift, conducted in such a way that no one else saw, but Freddy was as stupidly thrilled as if Adam had chartered a skywriter to fill the sky with ADAM + FREDDY.

"You ready?" His voice had gone gravelly.

"Yeah." Adam smiled, and they set out like always, and soon they were grinning at each other like dorks as they strolled. There were probably cartoon hearts and songbirds flitting around their heads.

But then something drew Adam's attention, and the smile slid off his face as he craned his neck to see something over Freddy's shoulder.

Freddy turned. Rusty Anderson—in his Lady Merlot persona—was coming out of the drugstore across the street.

"Let's drive," Adam said suddenly.

"What?"

"You have your car somewhere, right?"

"Uh, yeah. It's back at Miller's." Was Freddy imagining things, or was Adam trying to avoid Rusty?

They were both out, and Rusty was gay. Unlike Adam's family, he'd never had any issue with Adam being gay. So that left Freddy wondering: was Adam was embarrassed to be seen with Freddy because he was...Freddy?

No, that had to be wrong. Adam wasn't like that.

"I was just thinking, um..."

"Yeah?" Freddy prompted.

Adam waggled his eyebrows. "If we drove, we'd get there sooner."

A bolt of lust—tinged with no small amount of relief—shot through Freddy. He dug his keys out of his pocket. "Let's go."

Present day

Thirty minutes after the incident, Lulu was being loaded into an ambulance. The paramedics had bandaged a gash on her head—but not before, to her utter mortification, shaving a section of it—and pronounced her most likely fine. But she'd hit her head pretty hard on the dock as she'd fallen, and they thought it best for her to spend the night in the hospital to be monitored for a concussion.

"Henry!" Lulu cried. She'd been borderline hysterical after her "fall"—Freddy still had his doubts about the accidental nature of the event—and now it appeared she was ramping up again. "Henry! Ride with me." Freddy felt a little bad. The fact that she'd stopped hitting on him and wanted her brother with her suggested that even if the accident hadn't been genuine, the resulting distress was.

After some logistical discussion, it was decided that Henry would ride with Lulu in the ambulance and Mark and Chloe would follow, Mark driving Henry's car so it could be left at the hospital for when Henry needed it.

"Adam and I will meet you at the main entrance," Chloe said to Mark, clearly assuming she was taking her brother-in-law with her.

Adam looked at Freddy.

"If you'd rather walk," Freddy said, "I'll walk with you. I could use some fresh air." Never mind that they'd all been gulping fresh air all evening as the drama unfolded outside.

"I'd rather walk," Adam said shyly.

"It's going to take you forever!" Chloe rolled her eyes. "You are such a freak." But she must have been used to this quirk of his because she said no more, merely made her good-byes, and then she and Mark were off, leaving Ben, Adam, and Freddy alone in front of the house.

"Will you come in and let your hair dry and have a drink before you set out?" Ben asked.

Freddy was surprised when Adam agreed. He was usually only up for a limited amount of socializing, and this evening had been…a lot, even for Freddy, who had learned, in his years in the restaurant business, how to turn on the gregariousness despite his essential misanthropy. But Ben and Adam seemed to have genuinely hit it off earlier, which continued to gratify Freddy.

Inside, Ben poured three glasses of whiskey. He handed one to Adam, saying, "I think something stronger than wine is called for," and went to the fireplace. Soon he had a crackling fire burning and had lured Adam, who'd changed into some of Ben's clothing, over to sit beside it.

It was a tidy little scene, Adam wearing Ben's clothing, accepting a drink from him with murmured thanks. Once again, Freddy reminded himself that Ben was one hundred percent straight.

Not that that was relevant. Even if Ben had been making a move on Adam—which he *wasn't*—it was of no interest to Freddy.

"Well, isn't this very cozy and nineteenth-century?" Adam joked. "Drying my hair by the fire."

Ben smiled. "After a barely averted tragedy involving an ill-timed swoon."

"If only we'd had smelling salts, we might not have needed paramedics," Adam quipped.

"Too bad there isn't a yard full of turnips to pick. The monotony would probably calm our nerves."

Freddy attempted not to find it cute when both men erupted into laughter at what must haven been an inside joke.

Ben and Adam had a lot in common besides the fact that they were both bookworms. They each had a dry sense of humor and a fierce intelligence, both of which they kept close to their chests. Freddy thought again that it was probably no accident that he'd been attracted to them both—to Ben as a friend and to Adam as…everything.

God, as much as he didn't want it, all that attraction was back. It wasn't just physical attraction, though Adam's dark good looks were as potent as ever. It was the way Adam just… sucked up all his attention. His awareness. When he was in the room, Freddy was exquisitely aware of every move Adam made. Of his posture, and as impossible as it seemed, his mood. Even after all these years, he could tell, from the slight shifting of his weight, when his leg was bothering him. Or when he was biting his tongue to keep from saying something snarky to his brother or sister-in-law.

For God's sake, he'd almost cut off his finger at one point during the dinner prep because he'd been so distracted by Adam. It was exhausting.

Which is why it made no sense that he'd signed up to walk two hours round trip with him.

"You sure I can't run you home?" Ben asked.

"Thanks, but no. I'm a devoted pedestrian."

"You always were." As much as Adam had hurt him, Freddy couldn't help liking how that hadn't changed.

"Yeah," Adam said. "And you were always so nice to walk me home back in the day, but I'm really okay on my own."

"Wait. What?" Ben's brow furrowed. Yeah, Freddy had never told Ben about his…thing with Adam back in the day. He wasn't really sure why. Adam had been out, as had Freddy. Most people in town apparently hadn't known he was bisexual though—as evidenced by how surprised they had all apparently been by the "coming out" episode of *Food Fanatics*.

His family and Ben had definitely known he was into both girls and guys, though, and they were cool with it. They never talked about it explicitly, but Freddy got the feeling that Adam hadn't told anyone about them back then, and he'd followed his lead, even if he'd sometimes had to swallow the uncomfortable sense that maybe Adam was hiding him.

He'd rationalized shoving down those occasional moments of discomfort because their romance had been so intense that it had felt...private. Like it was for them only.

But eventually, he'd wanted more. Tried to force things as the summer drew to an end.

And had lost everything in the process.

"Yeah, um..." Adam clearly hadn't realized Ben didn't know about his past with Freddy. "Freddy used to walk me home sometimes when we both worked at Miller's Inn."

"Did he now?" Ben darted a glance at Freddy, a glance that suggested there would be an interrogation later.

All right. That was his cue. He stood. "You ready?"

"Let the man finish his drink," Ben protested.

"It's all right." Adam tipped his head back to do just that. "I'm done."

"Text if you want me to come get you at any point," Ben called after him as they headed down the driveway.

By the time they entered Uppercross and approached Adam's street, Freddy was much calmer. The walk had been a mix of not-uncomfortable silence and real conversation.

When they reached the motorhome, Freddy asked, "Did your family kick you out of the house? Is that why you moved into this thing?" As much as he wanted to hate Adam, the impulse to kick the ass of anyone who had mistreated him was strong this evening.

"Oh, no. After my dad died, I just...couldn't take living under the same roof as my mom and Betsy anymore. It was like he was a buffer for them, both personality-wise and financially. And then once he was gone..."

"It did not enable the angels of their better nature?"

Adam chuckled. "It did not."

"Good. Well, not good, but I've been wondering if she kicked you to the curb. I know she wasn't thrilled when you came out."

"Yeah, but she got over that. And once it became clear I wasn't the sort of homosexual she wanted, she mostly left me alone—when it came to that, anyway. She still hates my hair. And my freckles."

Freddy knew Adam's family had kicked him out and then relented, but they'd never really talked openly about his relationship with his mother. Freddy had been able to infer everything he needed to know from that horrible dinner. "What sort of homosexual did she want?"

"You know, one like she used to see on that straight-guy makeover show. Someone stylish." He held a hand up in front of his face the way people did when they were admiring a ring or a new manicure. "It's too dark to see, but I pretty much have grease permanently under my fingernails."

Why was that...so hot?

Freddy generally didn't go for the working-class hero type. His hookups in the city tended to be customers, who, given they were eating at his restaurant, were well-off.

They'd reached the door to the RV. "You think Lulu's okay?" Adam asked.

"I'm sure we'd have heard if she wasn't." Freddy paused, unsure if he should say the rest. Well, fuck it. "You did a good thing back there, saving her."

JENNY HOLIDAY

"Eh. I didn't save her. She would have been fine. She was two feet from the dock."

"Still. You kept your head. That was more than the rest of us can say. She's lucky you were there."

Adam continued to deflect the praise. "This will be the best thing that happens to Lulu all summer. She'll get so much mileage out of it."

"She's...something."

"Yeah, she, uh, seems fond of you."

Freddy chuckled. "You think?"

"I do. You're exactly her type."

"What's her type?" He couldn't resist asking. What qualities did Adam think Lulu saw in him?

"Rich. Famous."

"I'm hardly famous." He couldn't deny the rich part.

"Well, you're the highest profile person ever to come out of this town, and Lulu has to work with what she has. Say what you will about her, she's resourceful. I mean, jumping into the lake?"

"Yes! She *did* jump, right?"

"Seems like it."

Vindication! He hadn't been imagining that she'd done it on purpose. But he did sort of feel bad that her stunt was so obvious that everyone had seen through it. "Well, one thing I will say about Lulu McGuire is she keeps things interesting."

Adam blinked a few times, and Freddy had the strange sense that he was trying to cover up his true expression. He found himself desperately curious about what that expression would have been.

"You want me to drive you back to Ben's?" Adam asked.

"Can I use your bathroom?" Suddenly, Freddy wanted to see inside Adam's RV. If he couldn't see what was going on inside Adam's head, he wanted to see inside his home. Enough to manipulate his way in there apparently, because normally, outside and under the cover of darkness, the side of a tree was good enough for him.

"Uh, sure." Adam unlocked the door and held it for Freddy. "Light's just to your right. Beware the—"

Freddy was almost bowled over a flying mass of...not fur exactly. More like a compact bundle of skin-covered bones that leaped on him in a flurry of licking and high-pitched barking.

"—dog." Adam raised his voice. "Mr. Collins! Out."

The little mutt, apparently satisfied he had adequately greeted them, jumped down from the RV and trotted happily out into the yard.

Freddy flipped on the lights, and *holy shit*. "This place is *incredible*."

From the outside, Adam's place looked like your basic RV. But in here it was like a Pinterest page come to life. From Freddy's vantage point, he could see all the way down the RV. There were no walls or dividers—it was one big open space. They had entered just past the kitchen, which was close to one end. At the far side on the other end was a huge bed tucked against some windows. Next came a sitting area with a table, then the kitchen, where they were. But the most amazing thing was how the place was decorated. Freddy's overwhelming first impression was that there were plants everywhere—on most surfaces and packed along a shallow shelf that lined almost the entire space a foot or so from the ceiling. Some of them were twined with tiny white lights—like Christmas lights but smaller—that made the place feel like a fairy garden. "Wow." He walked farther in. Most RVs Freddy had been in or had seen pictures of were dull—browns, grays, sturdy synthetic fabric, imitation wood. Here, the kitchen cabinets were painted a sky blue that, along with all the greenery, brought to mind lake and sky. There was a tiny vintage Formica table edged in silver flanked by booth-like seating upholstered in a crazy floral pattern made up mostly of lime green but also with some of the same blue as on the cabinets.

It was cozy and, though Freddy didn't usually use words like this, uplifting. It was also so very...Adam. It perfectly exemplified Adam's hidden depths, the rich, beautiful interior he rarely showed people.

Freddy was as bowled over as he had been by the dog. "It's almost like you're outside."

"That's kind of what I was going for."

Freddy turned. The end of the RV behind him—which was the front—contained, of course, the driver's seat and a passenger seat. They were turned around to create a sort of reading nook. There was an end table slotted in between the chairs. It held a lamp and a stack of books. In the space above this tableau was a sort of loft that contained a small library lined with what had to be custom-made shelves, painted the same sky blue as the kitchen cabinetry.

"That's new," Adam said, following Freddy's gaze. "I used to have a double bed up there above the cab."

"For guests?" Which of course made Freddy think about the circumstances under which Adam would have guests. Although in his uncomfortable imaginings, the guests probably did not sleep in the spare bed.

"In theory. But it never actually got used."

Because your guests sleep in the other bed with you? The big one I can see down at the other end?

"So when we, uh, lost Kellynch, I built this little library." Adam gestured at the books. "I used to keep most of my books in the house, but..."

But my sister displaced you.

God, the onslaught of crappy emotions reminded Freddy why he didn't do relationships. Adam had been his first and only. After Adam, he'd reverted to form, keeping his liaisons casual. He was comfortable with casual.

"I ended up leaving the winemaking books there, though. I had no use for them, and I secretly hoped that whoever bought the place might decide to get it up and running again."

"I think they're a bit overwhelmed right now. But I wouldn't discount it eventually. My sister's very entrepreneurial."

"So she's been in Rochester all this time?"

"Yep. She was an Avon lady."

"They still have those?"

"They do. She did really well." He was proud of his sister —and himself. In their own ways, both Freddy and Sophie had done the proverbial bootstrap thing, creating a better life for themselves than they'd had as kids. They'd been able to help their mom, too, who, though Sophie had invited her to come live at Kellynch, preferred to stay in the apartment in Rochester to which she'd retired. Freddy did another scan of the space. "So books and nature, basically."

Adam laughed. "Yeah, I guess that pretty much sums me up."

"I bet when this was parked up against the forest at Kellynch, you really felt like you were in the woods."

"I definitely slept better there than I do here."

Something twisted in Freddy's chest at the image of Adam, curled up in his bed in the forest, lit only by the warm glow of the fairy lights. And then twisted *harder* when he thought of him *unable* to sleep, tossing restlessly in the same bed, not close enough to the trees for his mind to settle.

"Anyway, bathroom's there." Adam pointed to a small door.

Right. Freddy went in and peed a bit, even though he didn't really have to. When he came out, Adam was sitting at the little dinette table, resting his head in his hands.

"You must be exhausted." Jesus, what an evening.

"Yeah, I think I was going on pure adrenaline for a while there, and now I'm crashing." His stomach rumbled audibly, and he laughed. "I don't know how I can be hungry after that amazing meal."

"Well, since dinner, you've only jumped in a lake to save someone's life, overseen an emergency, and walked for an hour and fifteen minutes." Adam started to get up, but Freddy held up a hand. "Stay there. Let me bring you something." He turned to the small refrigerator. "You mind?"

"Nope, but you're not going to find much in there. Unlike you, I'm not much of a cook."

Hmm. He was right. There were some condiments, a few bottles of beer, a single apple, and... "Cheese. Do you have bread? I make a pretty mean grilled cheese."

"In the breadbox on the counter. But you don't have to—"

"Shh." He did have to, was the thing. He might still half hate Adam, but damn, he could never stand to see him suffer. "I'm starving, too." That was true. And he hadn't even jumped in a lake.

In keeping with the vintage theme, Adam had a midcentury enamel breadbox. Freddy extracted some good-looking bread that appeared to be from the local bakery and sliced the cheddar from the fridge as well as the apple. "It's kind of fun cooking in here."

"I suppose you're used to huge kitchens."

"Restaurant kitchens are actually pretty small, especially if you consider how much food is moving through them."

"But on your show—"

Freddy turned. Adam was doing the blushing-while-looking-at-the-floor thing. Damn, the idea that Adam had watched that stupid show. That he remembered stuff from it. But he didn't want Adam to be embarrassed so he just said, dismissively, "That was reality TV, not reality."

"So that kitchen on the episode where you went to that barbecue place in Memphis was not representative?"

Damn, he *had* watched. He bit back a grin as he plopped some butter into a pan he'd put on the small single burner in the little kitchen. "Nope. That was a freakishly large kitchen. My place in New York has a much smaller kitchen. Though that's partly reflective of the cost of real estate in Manhattan."

"I was surprised to see you on TV. We all were."

"I did that show to get Ben off my back. Since pretty much the moment we left this town, he got nostalgic for it. When the house he now owns came on the market, he became obsessed with it, but he needed a quick infusion of cash to be able to buy it."

"So you sold your soul to the TV devil so Ben could come home?"

Freddy chuckled. "Pretty much. We'd been interviewed a bunch on a local network in New York, and eventually became a regular segment on the local morning show. We sort of developed this shtick—although it wasn't a shtick, it was pretty much just us—whereby he was always enthusiastic and optimistic about everything and I was the cranky asshole." He shrugged. "It worked, so they dialed it up for the show. We only did the one show ourselves, but we still have the production company—we develop other shows, which is where the money really comes from on an ongoing basis. I mean the restaurant does fine, too, but…"

Was it weird to be talking about money with Adam, who'd just lost his home?

"How come you called the restaurant Captain's if it's both yours and Ben's?"

People were always asking him that. "No reason, really, other than that the menu is seafood-heavy, and the designer we hired wanted to do a retro, seafood-shack sort of aesthetic. So Captain's seemed kind of cute."

"And you were happy to have Ben's name be on it and not yours."

People were always asking him that, too, like they couldn't believe an asshole like Freddy would be okay with that decision. Honestly, he hadn't given it any thought. He figured he and Ben knew food, but that they should take the advice of the experts on the rest of it—as much as he wished it could be all about the food, that other shit mattered in the restaurant business.

Adam wasn't asking it as a question, though. It had been a sentence, one he followed with a nod, like he was confirming to himself his interpretation of the situation. It stung a little, because it reminded him how Adam had always seen him in a truer way than everyone else had, and how buoying it had been to be seen like that.

But this was not a productive train of thought. They needed to talk about something else.

"Hang on. Are you putting *mayo* on those grilled cheeses?" Adam curled his lip, and Freddy tried not to find it adorable even as he was grateful for the change of subject that had arrived just as he'd wished for it.

"I am. Secret ingredient."

"Sounds pretty disgusting to me."

"Just you wait." He plopped the first sandwich, the outside slathered with mayo, in the bubbling butter.

Ten minutes later, his efforts were rewarded when Adam bit into his sandwich and said, through a mouthful, "This is amazing."

Freddy smirked and tried his own. It was good. This was what he liked about cooking, the way you could take simple ingredients and make them into something more than the sum of their parts. You could subvert expectations. It had been a long time since he'd made something as simple as a grilled cheese, though. He'd kind of missed it. Maybe they should put one on the fall menu at Captain's. He had no doubt that sophisticated New Yorkers would embrace it in a high-low sort of way, but something didn't sit right about serving grilled cheese in an ironic way. It was too easy—it felt cynical, almost. Though when had he had ever worried about being overly cynical?

"I never would have thought of putting apple slices in a grilled cheese," Adam said after his first bite.

"Standard grilled cheese hack. So is the mayo. It makes the bread get all perfectly golden and crispy on the outside."

"Nothing about this tastes standard." Adam took another bite. "This would be so good with my dad's pinot. Hang on." He moved to get up. Freddy wanted to insist that he not, wanted to offer to bring him the wine—or anything he wanted, really—but he checked himself. That wasn't his role anymore.

Soon, Adam was back with a bottle and two stemless glasses. "I think maybe the fruitiness of the apple will be good with this."

Adam splashed some of the ruby liquid into Freddy's glass,

and Freddy took a sip. "I think you're right." It was a good pairing.

They drank and ate in silence for a few minutes. Then Adam said, "This is the last bottle."

"What do you mean the last bottle?"

"The last time we harvested grapes at Kellynch was the year my dad died. The pinot was the best wine from that year, and this is the last bottle."

Freddy physically pushed his glass away. "Shit, man. You should be saving it."

"For what, though? I'm not exactly a social butterfly."

"I don't know. You should at least, like, go outside and lay on the ground and look at the stars and toast your dad while you drink it."

"I don't need to go outside for that." Adam got up, switched off the kitchen light, and walked over to the bed. Amazingly, it was a king-size. It fully filled the nook it was tucked into, was flush against three walls. So he had to back up into it—sit down and sort of scoot backward. He patted the mattress next to him.

Uh, what?

As if he could read Freddy's mind, Adam chuckled. "Just come here. I want to show you something."

Freddy could suddenly think of a lot of things he would enjoy seeing in Adam's bed, but he was pretty sure those weren't the things Adam was planning to show him. Warily, he obeyed, mimicking Adam's action in backing himself into the nook. It was insanely cozy, to be tucked into a contained space like this. There were walls on both sides, and the back of the space, where the headboard would have been, was a series of windows.

Adam pointed at the ceiling.

"Oh!" It was studded with stars. Like those glow-in-the-dark ones you see in kids' rooms, except somehow less childish. Instead of greenish dots, the stars were white, and blurry around the edges. There were also some planets, and a swath of overlapping stars approximating the milky way. "This is amazing." It almost took his breath away.

This was the thing about Adam. He had this secret...heart. On the surface of things, he was reserved, practical, even unremarkable. But underneath that, he was quietly devoted to beauty. Real beauty, though, not the superficial kind. The kind that could lodge a lump in your throat that took a really long time to go away.

Adam twisted around and opened one of the windows. "You were right about Kellynch. When I slept with the windows open there, I could hear all the sounds of the forest. Here, it's more muted."

Freddy cocked an ear. There were crickets, and a breeze—which weren't nothing. He didn't get those in the city. But he understood what Adam was saying. "It must have been almost like sleeping outside."

"Yep. *Almost* being the key word, though. Both my sisters are always telling me that I should just actually sleep outside."

"Oh, no. Do they know you?" Despite being a nature freak, Adam had always liked his creature comforts. It was no accident this was an insanely fluffy king-size bed.

But, then, did *Freddy* know Adam? He used to—he'd thought. But he hadn't really, had he?

"Exactly." Adam flopped back on his pillows and sighed contentedly. "This mattress cost more than I care to admit."

"And what do you do about baths?" That was another thing Freddy remembered about Adam—he loved taking long, hot baths. He didn't know this firsthand—he'd never been lucky enough back in the day to share a bath with Adam. Just that they used to talk about it when they would emerge from the moonlit lake late at night, shivering. Adam used to tease Freddy that he had to walk back to town while Adam would go inside and get in the bath. But then, being Adam, the joking would turn to fretting as he'd start genuinely worrying over the long, cold, solitary walk ahead of Freddy. He'd press a flower on him and hug him like he never wanted to let go. Freddy's throat started to ache. Instead of dissipating, that stupid lump was getting bigger.

"That's the one big drawback of this place," Adam said, oblivious to the twinging of Freddy's heart. "It only has a small shower stall. At Kellynch, I used to take baths in the house, but..."

And once again, he trailed off, leaving Freddy to complete the sentence with *my sister displaced you.*

Freddy didn't say it out loud, of course. He didn't know *what* to say. So he just laid there looking at the ceiling of stars and trying to get a goddamn hold on himself.

CHAPTER TEN

Eight years ago

Adam never understood why everyone was always talking about how rough and unrefined Freddy was. Freddy paid attention. His regard contained concentration and urgency but also patience and kindness. His ministrations were always perfectly pitched.

"Oh, my God!" Adam had been trying to be quiet, but it slipped out. They were on the dock, and it was after midnight, but still. There was no precedent for it, but the last thing he needed was for someone in his family to wake up, wander down, and find him buck naked and flat on his back on the dock with Freddy Wentworth's lips wrapped around his dick. Adam had no doubt that his family would kick him out again if they found out he was carrying on with Freddy Wentworth. And this time, Rusty wouldn't be there to cushion his landing.

Freddy popped off and kneeled up. Gilded with moonlight and grinning mischievously, he looked like he'd stepped from the pages of *A Midsummer Night's Dream*, like he was enchanted, profoundly unconcerned by the bounds of propriety or the strictures of reality.

"Shh." Laughingly, he pressed a hand lightly over Adam's mouth.

Nodding, Adam placed both his hands over Freddy's.

They stared at each other for a long time, Freddy's smile gradually disappearing. He looked at Adam like he was seeing him for the first time. Like he wanted to memorize him. But then, suddenly, the grin came back, and he said, "You'll have to let go of my hand if you want me to finish the job."

Adam's hands came away like Freddy's was a hot stove.

Freddy chuckled. "I thought so."

And after he had *finished the job*, and after Adam had recip-rocated, they stretched out on the dock, Freddy on his back, Adam in his arms and half draped over his chest, and looked at the stars.

Freddy played with Adam's hair and let him ramble about the constellations. And then when he was done, he let Adam straddle him and...examine him. That was the only word for it, really. It was probably weird, but Adam loved this almost as much as their actual lovemaking. He would start by smoothing his hands over Freddy's chest, and then he would move to his biceps, one at a time, ending on the side with the Celtic tattoo, stroking it and staring at it like it was the first time he was seeing it.

He always paused at a scar on the side of Freddy's torso that was angry enough to be seen even in the dim illumination provided by the moon and by their lantern. Freddy'd gotten it running away from a cop, he'd said, when he'd climbed a fence intending to jump down on the other side but instead fell onto a sharp rock.

Continuing with his carnal inventory, Adam would then

slide his fingers over the bump that was the remnant of a nose break that had occurred as part of a schoolyard scuffle, the one piece of Freddy's face that wasn't theoretically perfect. Paradoxically, to Adam, that so-called flaw made Freddy even more beautiful.

Finally, he would twist a wooden ring Freddy wore on his right middle finger. It was a smooth, dark wooden band that he'd made in shop class before he'd quit school, and Adam loved the feel of it under his fingers. Twisting it soothed him, profoundly.

It was probably a weird ritual, but to Adam it seemed like taking stock, reminding himself anew that this amazing person, with all his adornments and his single imperfection, was his. It didn't hurt that Freddy seemed to like it, too. He'd close his eyes sometimes and smile and sort of hum low in his throat, like Adam's ministrations felt good. There was also the part where his dick would get hard again—that hadn't been Adam's aim, at least to begin with, but it was an amazing side effect, knowing he had that much power over a man like Freddy.

Eventually, Freddy would put a stop to the slow, teasing touching. Like tonight, when his hands shot up and grabbed Adam's wrists. Tugged on them until Adam was lying on top of him, and he said, "Enough?"

"Enough?" Adam echoed laughingly as he ground his hips against Freddy's. "Or not enough?"

Freddy groaned. "Both."

Present day

123

Adam awoke the next morning wedged right up against the wall. He always did that. He was a burrower. He had an entire king-size bed to himself, but he always managed to migrate in his sleep over to the wall and—

Hold on.

Hold *on*.

That wasn't a wall he was curled up next to. It was a warm, human body.

Freddy. Freddy, who was sleeping on his side facing Adam, his top arm slung over Adam.

A wave of emotion—of truth—bore down on Adam. It came in several parts. The first was joy. *Freddy. Freddy is here. I'm in Freddy's arms.* It was like before, but not. The eight years since Adam had last found himself here had hardened Freddy's body. He'd bulked out. Not hugely, but enough that the arm over his torso felt heavier than it used to. And where he used to be clean shaven, modern-day Freddy seemed to perpetually sport several days' worth of stubble. That scruff seemed to Adam a wondrous thing. He wanted to touch it. To let his fingertips drag over it. To let his *lips* drag over it.

He'd given up the right to do that, though.

And then the wave moved on, and fear displaced joy. What would happen when Freddy woke up? What would happen when Freddy left—both Adam's bed and Bishop's Glen? Adam's skin started to tingle, and not in a good way. His breath grew short. He had to concentrate to keep it inaudible. He wasn't really sure what was happening to him, only that he must not wake Freddy.

He closed his eyes, feeling like if he pretended to be asleep, he could somehow keep Freddy here. It was irrational. But maybe not, because after a few moments of concentrating on evening out his breath, the fear abated.

And then came the sadness. The knowledge that Freddy *would* wake up. He *would* leave. And that was worse, way worse, than if he'd never been here—in Adam's bed or in Bishop's Glen—at all.

Last night, Adam had allowed himself to fantasize about what that dinner party would have been like if he and Freddy were still a couple. It would have been him, not Lulu, flirting with Freddy in the kitchen—Adam and Freddy alone together in the crowd. His fantasy hadn't gone any further than that, though. It was like his brain simply hadn't been capable of contemplating what might have come next, after dinner.

It hadn't been able to contemplate *this*.

Waking up in Freddy's arms in his beloved little home.

It wasn't even a sexual thing, necessarily. Yes, he was sporting more than his usual degree of morning wood, and that wasn't a coincidence, but the thing about Freddy was Adam's attraction to him had always been more than sexual. It had been about this. About being close. About sharing the mundane details of daily life. He'd loved Freddy so very, very much.

Which was probably why Rusty had freaked out so extremely. He'd been able to sense it, somehow.

Adam thought he'd grieved Freddy. And he *had*. That first year after Freddy left town was a blur. He had only vague memories of Rusty nagging him, always nagging him, to leave town, to apply to college. Of helping his dad at Kellynch, trying in vain to get him to trust him with more responsibility. Of his mother fruitlessly attempting to mold him into a gay male version of Betsy, as if to round out a collection of acolytes. Of trying to break the spell Freddy still had over him with those few ill-fated hookups. Through it all, he'd been sad. So sad.

But he'd had *no idea*. He hadn't really known what he'd been missing. Before Freddy left, the future had been this theoretical thing pulling him in different directions. Stay in town. Leave. Try to convince Dad to let him learn the ropes at the winery. Give up and be a mechanic. But before Freddy left, none of it had seemed that urgent, because at that point, all of those futures had contained Freddy.

Until they hadn't.

Now, though, this morning, he *knew*. The future he could have had was no longer theoretical. Regardless of what else he could have decided—about jobs, about where to live, about whether to go to college—he could have had *this*. He could have woken up every morning in Freddy Wentworth's arms.

And, oh God, it *hurt*. It filled his throat with razors and his guts with poison.

Regret was such an innocuous word. It rolled off the tongue so easily, two soft, round syllables that sounded almost chipper. Like it didn't have the power to encompass much beyond *I regret not having ordered the chicken. I regret that the rain has ruined our picnic.*

In truth, *regret* was a sly, nasty sucker. So big. So heavy.

He rolled over. He tried to do it as quietly as possible, because for some nonsensical, suicidal reason, he *still* didn't want Freddy to wake up and leave, but he had to turn his head away, because tears were starting.

He could tell the moment Freddy awakened. He thought he'd made it. Had moved onto his stomach and turned his head to face the wall, and Freddy's breathing had kept coming in the same steady, deep pattern. But then it stopped, just for a moment. You had to be paying close attention to hear it, but Adam had been. The quality of the arm that still rested on his body changed. It tightened ever so slightly. You had to be paying close attention to feel it, but, again, Adam been.

The words came a breath later. "Oh, my God. I fell asleep." And then the arm started to pull away. The warm chest began to recede. "Shit. I'm sorry."

Adam wanted to wail. He checked the impulse, but another one arrived immediately on its heels: *what if I kissed him?*

What if, instead of passively letting the joy-fear-sadness wave subsume him, he, uncharacteristically, *did what he wanted?* What if the future he'd been imagining, and mourning, was something he could just reach out and take?

Before he could overthink things, he turned over, heart pounding with a mixture of fear and hope and exhilaration, and rested his hand on top of Freddy's. Without making eye contact, he pulled Freddy's arm back over him. After some initial resistance, it came. Settled. Maybe not as heavily as before—could an arm be wary?—but it was there.

Okay, this was it. In order to kiss a man you hadn't kissed in years, you had to look at him. You had to make sure he was okay with it. Adam willed his eyes not to leak as he raised them.

Freddy was shocked. He looked like a surprised-face emoji, his eyes and mouth round. But he wasn't pulling away.

So, feeling like this might be the bravest thing he would ever do, Adam lifted his head some more and extended his neck. He wanted to pounce on Freddy, like that first time he'd kissed him at the foot of the drive at Kellynch, so impulsively and suddenly. But since he still wasn't sure *this* kiss was welcome, he forced himself to move slowly, to make his intentions clear while still allowing space for retreat.

He must have been moving too slowly, though, because

Freddy, his surprise vanishing so thoroughly Adam wondered if he'd imagined it to begin with, let loose a low growl and took over, closing the space between them. His lips hit Adam's at the same time his hand slid along the back of Adam's skull, anchoring him for what was to come.

And then he was *kissing Freddy Wentworth*. Again. Still. It was at once as if no time had passed but also not at all like that, because this time he knew what this was worth. How rare this was.

On a sigh, Adam let his jaw go slack, inviting Freddy farther in. Freddy didn't hesitate, just swept his tongue inside Adam's mouth on a groan, with that firm-but-soft touch that was so uniquely Freddy. Adam wanted this kiss to go on forever. To never end, because—

"Shit."

All Freddy had done was pull away, but it felt like a seam ripping, like a lifetime of careful, incremental stitching had been ruthlessly yanked out, exposing ugly, ragged edges.

Freddy rolled away from Adam so rapidly he hit the wall. Bonked his head audibly.

"I'm sorry," Adam said at the same time Freddy, raking his hands through his hair, said, "We can't do this."

"I know. I know. I don't know what I was thinking." It was a lie, though. He'd been thinking, for one irrational, buoying moment, that maybe he could have what he wanted. That maybe there were such things as second chances. "I'm so sorry."

Freddy ignored Adam's apology. He crab-walked forward on the mattress—there really was no graceful way to get in or out of Adam's bed—and heaved himself up. It was like he couldn't get off the bed fast enough. "What time is it?"

He was headed toward the kitchen table where he'd left his

phone, so clearly the question wasn't aimed at Adam specifically, but, having no idea what else to say, Adam answered it anyway. "Judging from the sound of the birds, I'd say just before six."

Freddy picked up his phone and squinted at it.

"Well, Grizzly Adam—pun intended—you're exactly right. It's five-fifty." Though Freddy had made a joke, there was no warmth in his tone. No accompanying wink like Adam used to get back in the day.

Adam followed Freddy off the bed. This had all been a mistake. Not just the kiss, but showing Freddy the ceiling. The grilled cheese. Probably even going to the party in the first place. No good could come of any of it.

What had he been *thinking*? There would be no second chances for Adam.

And the universe must have decided to hammer home that point, because the next thing Freddy said was, "I have a text from Lulu."

Of course he did. In the weird haze that had overtaken Adam this morning, that had propelled him to kiss Freddy, he'd somehow managed to forget all about Lulu. "Is she okay?"

"I think so. They kept her overnight to watch her, but they're releasing her today. She wants me to go get her."

That didn't make any sense. Why wouldn't her parents or her brother or even Mark or Chloe, who lived across the street from her, pick her up? Why would she ask Freddy?

Well, he knew why, didn't he?

"But you know Lulu. I'm sure there will be some drama or other we don't know about yet." He smiled at the phone before shoving it in his back pocket. Adam very much feared it was an affectionate smile.

Freddy cleared his throat. "Anyway. Sorry I fell asleep on you."

Adam waved his hand dismissively. Freddy was not the one who should be apologizing. "No problem. And sorry again about that kiss. That was…epically stupid."

It was Freddy's turn to wave off Adam's words as he bent to put his shoes on. Adam had the sudden sense that by not acknowledging either of the apologies Adam had made, Freddy could pretend the kiss had never happened at all.

All right, then. Adam could take a hint. "You want me to run you back to Ben's?" He paused. "Or to the hospital?"

Stupidly, even after all that had gone down, even mired in this strange awkwardness, Adam still kind hoped Freddy would say yes. Fool that he was, he wanted to prolong their time together, even if that meant delivering Freddy to Lulu's bedside.

Freddy paused with his hand on the door. "No, no. I'm going to head back to Ben's to shower before going to get Lulu, but I'll walk, thanks." Freddy's lips turned up, but Adam wouldn't call the resulting expression a smile. "You must be rubbing off on me."

Adam lifted his hand in farewell and was in receipt of one of Freddy's curt nods, and that was that.

A few minutes later—he waited long enough to give Freddy a head start so he wouldn't think Adam was following him—he headed out himself. Mr. Collins had come back in the doggie door at some point during the night and was curled up on the RV's driver's seat snoring something fierce. He roused the little beast and clipped on his leash. Maybe walking into town for breakfast before work would help him get his head back into reality, into a world where he didn't get to just wake up in the morning and find Freddy there.

What he encountered did not help. A few minutes into his walk, he made a turn and was startled to find Freddy standing by the side of the road, looking at his phone. Reflexively, Adam darted behind a tree, and by some miracle, Mr. Collins remained silent.

What should he do? Very quietly turn around? But what if Mr. Collins decided to break his uncharacteristic silence, and Freddy saw them? It would be worse, would it not, to be seen slinking away than to be seen taking a walk in his own neighborhood? Taking a walk was a totally reasonable thing for a person—especially a person with a dog—to be doing.

His indecision kept him still, but then it didn't matter. A taxi pulled up, and Freddy got in. He hadn't wanted to walk, after all. He had called a taxi rather than accept a ride from Adam. And, worse, he hadn't even been able, apparently, to wait in Adam's RV for the cab to arrive.

A lump rose in Adam's throat, bitter and hard. Suddenly, he wished *he* could call a taxi and have it take him somewhere far away, out of this town with its tortures both large and small. It was the first time he had ever seriously been tempted by the idea of leaving Bishop's Glen.

He waited until the cab was out of sight, then stepped out from his hiding place, hunched his shoulders against the chilly dawn air, and set out. "Come on, Mr. Collins."

CHAPTER ELEVEN

Eight years ago

"Whose car is this?"

Adam stood from where he'd been crouched next to Freddy's Mustang. He was installing new brake pads.

"Good morning to you, too." When Rusty didn't say anything, Adam sighed and answered the question. "This is Freddy Wentworth's car."

"I thought so. And is anything wrong with it this time besides sabotage?"

Adam rolled his eyes, but warmth spread through him. Freddy had long since admitted that he *had* sabotaged his own car that day in the hopes of getting to spend time with Adam, but the thought of it still make Adam flush with pleasure.

"I assume you'll be charging him this time?"

"For the parts." Which wasn't true—he hadn't even been going to do that, but something told Adam that it was better to mislead Rusty a little here. "But not for the labor—that's why I came in early. I'm not on the clock yet."

Rusty didn't say anything. He didn't have to. Like Adam's mother, Rusty could convey an entire universe's worth of sentiment with the slightest movement of a nostril.

"What?" Adam asked, uncharacteristically pissy. Rusty's bad mood had chased off Adam's good one. Since Adam had been so happy lately, he'd started noticing he was sort of an emotional sponge around Rusty—he absorbed his friend's moods. He'd start out happy, and then after some time in Rusty's line of fire, he'd end up grumpy. He tried not to be so easily swayed, but he often couldn't help it.

"Nothing," Rusty said.

"It's not nothing. Why don't you just say what you think? You don't want me working on this car for free."

"I don't," Rusty snapped. "But there's a lot of things I don't want. For example, I don't want you here to begin with."

"Thanks a lot."

That softened Rusty. "Oh, you know what I mean. There's nothing *for* you here, except a shitty family."

"What about you?"

"A shitty family and an aging queen."

Adam snorted. It angered him that Rusty could be so dismissive about not only the town, but about his own importance in Adam's life.

"It's not too late to apply for spring admission," Rusty said. "To Cornell, even. You don't have to go that far away."

"I'd never get into Cornell." Adam had done okay in school, but he was far from Ivy League material. He could see Rusty ramping up his usual argument, but damn, he wasn't in the mood. He wanted to get his workday started. Because the sooner he started, the sooner he'd be done. Which meant the sooner he could drive Freddy's car back to him. The idea of hanging out with Freddy not in the middle of the night was… strangely thrilling. Of course hanging out with him in the middle of the night was thrilling, too. But they'd decided Adam would drop the car and then they'd grab some dinner.

It was almost like…a date.

He was stupidly nervous, though. Afraid, really. That someone would see them and come to the obvious conclusion and that the news would get back to his family. Or, worse, Rusty. But for once, uncharacteristically, his fear wasn't strong enough to hold him back. Who cared if Freddy was poor? A dropout? Those things weren't crimes. They weren't anything but labels everyone got hung up on. Rusty might be Adam's fairy godfather and all that, but he wasn't *actually* all knowing.

"Can we just skip the lecture? I don't know why it's so hard for you to understand that I *like* this town."

"What is there to like? What could possibly be keeping you here?"

That—that second question—was, at least, a new one.

"The lake" was his first answer. "The forests." He stuck out his tongue. "You, you jerk."

Rusty rolled his eyes. "Well, that goes without saying." Then he sobered. "As long as one of those things isn't Freddy Wentworth, then, yes, we can skip the lecture." He looked down his nose at the Mustang. "But if one of those things *is* Freddy Wentworth, I will be readying a whole new lecture, the likes of which you have never experienced."

Present day

By the time Rusty appeared in the shop that afternoon—Adam

135

had opened up—Adam had gotten a hold of himself. Tried to forget the morning's kiss, as he was sure Freddy, who was probably hanging out with Lulu even now, had already done.

Rusty, bearing coffees from the bakery, passed one to Adam and grinned. "I have the best idea."

"If it has anything do to with how to get Mrs. Littleton to understand that eventually, it doesn't make sense to keep fixing this sucker"—he kicked the tire of her LeSabre—"then I'm all ears." In truth, though, he could not complain about Mrs. Littleton's ancient Buick. He had been able to lose himself in the problem that was her engine cooling system, and in the process, recover his wits, which had taken quite a beating from the events of the morning.

"Let's go to the Hamptons."

Adam whipped his head up so rapidly that he smashed it on the edge of the propped-open hood. "Ow!"

Rusty ignored Adam's suffering. "Have you heard from your mother and sister?"

"A bit." No more than a text here or there. It had been a relief, actually, to be away from them. They were most likely embarrassing themselves and overstaying their welcome with Charlie, but he found that once they were out of sight, he could make himself not worry about it. And not worrying about it, while novel, had been surprisingly liberating.

Although, now that he thought about it, maybe he'd been *too* liberated. Had had too much time, in the vacuum created by his family's absence, to imagine a future that wasn't in his grasp.

"Don't you think you should go check on them?"

"Do *you*?" What was Rusty up to? If anything, he had always advocated for Adam to take *less* of an interest in his family, it being one more thing he believed was unjustly tying Adam to Bishop's Glen.

"Well, I have a friend in the Hamptons, you see."

"You *do*?"

Rusty was full of surprises today. Adam thought he knew all there was to know about Rusty—the man did not hide his light under a bushel. And for someone who complained about the smallness and small-mindedness of Bishop's Glen—and had made it his mission to catapult Adam out of town—he was certainly rooted in the place. Other than the odd cruise-ship vacation, he never went anywhere farther than Rochester.

"Yes, an old friend I've recently reconnected with on Facebook. I'd like to visit him."

"What about the shop?"

Rusty waved a hand. "Eh. We're allowed to take a vacation."

He suddenly realized what was going on. "This is about getting me away from Freddy Wentworth, isn't it?"

"What? No!"

"Rusty, you don't have to worry about Freddy and me. You already took care of that." Well, that wasn't entirely fair. All Rusty had done was express his opinion—forcefully and frequently. Adam needed to remember that although it was sometimes convenient to blame Rusty, he—Adam—was the one who'd spoken the words that sent Freddy away.

But before he could amend his accusation, Rusty said, "Yes, and I stand by that. You had a ton of potential."

Adam's heart raced. They had never spoken openly about Rusty's campaign to break up Adam and Freddy. "Which you somehow think I wasted working for you? Expanding your business?"

"Yes, I do. You had potential. You were just shit at actioning it, it turned out."

"And you were just shit at giving advice, it turned out."

Rusty's eyebrows shot up. Adam *never* spoke to Rusty like this. Well, hell. He didn't care. And now that he'd started, he couldn't seem to stop. "And now you want to do it again? Get me out of Freddy's notorious clutches? He's still not good enough for me, even though he did exactly what you were always after me to do—got the hell out of this town and made something of himself?"

Rusty stared at him silently for a long moment. "I simply suggested we take a vacation so you can check on your idiotic family and I can reconnect with an old friend." Ice formed around Rusty's words.

"What's this friend's name?"

"Harry Smith."

Adam barked an incredulous laugh.

"What, pray tell, is so amusing?"

"That's a fake name if I ever heard one. There isn't a friend." God, he'd forgotten how conniving Rusty could be when he had an active cause.

Rusty glared at Adam. "I'll have you know that Harry was in the restaurant business, just like your precious Freddy. He's newly retired, but he's got connections, and he thinks he can get me a guest run at a drag bar." He sniffed. "So I'll just go by myself."

Shit. Adam might have been experiencing an uncharacteristic flare of anger here, but the fact remained that Rusty was his best friend. The only person he could really rely on in this town—and hence, in the world. "Rusty, wait." Rusty paused halfway to the bay where his first car of the day was waiting but did not turn. He was hurt but trying not to show it.

"I'm sorry," Adam said quietly.

That was enough to get Rusty to turn around.

"I would actually love to get away for a while," he added. It was true. Even if Rusty's motivations were suspect, and even if it meant a return to having to deal with his mother and sister. Hadn't he just been wishing for a magical taxi to transport him out of town?

And hadn't the whole point of that wish been to spare himself the pain of being so near to Freddy? Of having to be constantly reminded of what he couldn't have?

So who cared how it got granted? And damn Rusty; he might actually be right about the wisdom of putting some distance between Adam and Freddy. This time. "Give me the dates, and I'll book my ticket tonight."

Rusty was clearly surprised by Adam's acquiescence but covered it quickly. "Flying's too much of a pain. We'd have to drive to Rochester, and then when we land, rent a car and drive out to Long Island. So we might as well just drive the whole way. I'm working on a pretty boy who will get us there in style." He jerked his head at his work bay.

"That's *yours*?" Adam had assumed it belonged to one of the wealthy summer people. While Rusty liked to drive in style, and had a collection of personal vehicles, the vintage red convertible was outlandish even for him.

He smirked. "It's a little red Miata."

"Shouldn't it be a little red Corvette?" Adam teased, glad they were back on friendly footing.

"Close enough."

CHAPTER TWELVE

Eight years ago

This might have been a mistake.

Freddy's whole modus operandi when it came to Adam was not to push. To let things unfold. To let it be easy, because it *was* easy.

Well, it was easy if you stripped away everything and everyone else. If they'd existed in a vacuum, which would have suited Freddy fine, honestly. His opinion about most people ranged from indifference to outright hostility.

It was just that he'd been starting to worry. A little bit. There was a hint of chill in the air when the sun went down. What was going to happen when they couldn't hang out for endless hours outside? So he'd been...not pushing exactly, but expressing little bits of what he was thinking. *It was fun that one time we went out to dinner—we should do that again. I wish I could see your freckles during the day.* Asking more questions about Adam's family, and about Rusty Anderson, who seemed to be more of a father to Adam than his own. Both because he genuinely wanted to know about the people in Adam's life, but also because he secretly wanted to probe a bit, to see if his fear that Adam was hiding Freddy from them was justified.

And his pushy not-pushing must have worked, because out of the blue, Adam invited him for dinner.

Which was why he was pulling up to Kellynch for the first time in a car. In the daylight—well, in the late August twilight, but close enough.

But the minute he walked in, he understood. If their relationship was going to work long term, he was going to have to get Adam away from his family.

Adam's relatives were...not like him. His mother and siblings were snobby, to begin with. The chill in the air was palpable as they offered him limp hands to shake. Adam was always raving about TV shows that ran on *Masterpiece Theatre*, and Freddy, wanting always to know Adam more and better, had watched one recently. This reminded him of it. It was like everyone was saying one thing but communicating another as they sat around and made pained conversation.

Adam's dad wasn't so bad. He was quiet, like Adam, and mostly drowned out by his wife and kids, but for a while, Freddy had gotten him talking animatedly about the vineyard. He watched Adam come to life, too, during this conversation. Adam had told Freddy about his wish to take over when his dad retired—and also that his dad had good-naturedly rebuffed all his attempts to help with the grapes or the wine-making. It was hard to fathom what was going on in his father's mind. Clearly neither of the other two siblings had any interest in anything beyond their own noses. He tried probing a little bit, asking questions he knew Adam could answer to try to paint him in a good light. But it wasn't long before Wilhelmina, whom he'd come to understand was the head of the family in every way that mattered, redirected the conversation.

He excused himself to go to the bathroom at one point. On his way back, he lingered for a moment in the hallway, looking at the family pictures hanging there but also just catching his breath, when she appeared.

"I have a lovely family, don't I?"

She stood in the narrow corridor with one scarlet-tipped hand on each wall, blocking the way back to the dining room.

Freddy pasted a smile on his face. "You do."

An uncomfortable silence descended. He felt like she was trying to see into his soul, and irrationally, like she might be able to do it.

And possibly also steal it.

"I get the sense, Freddy Wentworth, that you're not the sort of man who appreciates platitudes."

"Uh…" Shit. What was happening? He had no idea what to say.

"So I'm just going to say what I have to say, which is *stay away from my son.*"

"*Excuse* me?" Well, there. That had come out sounding confrontational and pissy, but at least he'd found his voice. He'd tried to be on his best behavior this evening, but still, he was not interested in or accustomed to being cowed. He might not have as much money, or education, as the Elliots, but that didn't mean he didn't have his pride.

But, okay. He needed to think strategically. He needed to not let his anger show. He couldn't make a scene right now. He couldn't put Adam in that position if he had any hope of creating something lasting with him. So as difficult as it was, he schooled his expression to a mild bewilderment, smiled, and said, "You say that like I'm after him romantically."

"And aren't you?"

"Of course not."

Wilhelmina pursed her lips. She was a smart woman. She had no doubt heard about the town square incident. She knew how to put two and two together.

Freddy smiled placidly. "Adam and I are just friends."

Freddy wasn't the type to get himself worked up over lying. He'd manufactured a lot of fake sick notes back in his school days, and he regularly promised his mother he was studying for his GED, which he most decidedly was not. But to say those words? *We're just friends.* Something inside him died a little, something fragile but *alive* he hadn't even been aware of. And even as it was gasping for breath, it raised a hand and said, *No!*

He is mine.

He quashed that part. Killed it conclusively. If he wanted it to be true, he had to get out of this situation. Sometimes you had to make a strategic retreat in the name of winning the larger war. The Elliots would have to be confronted at some point, but not by him and not now.

Wilhelmina tapped her long nails on the walls. "Even so, I think you can appreciate that there is a certain...social gap between you and my son. Regardless of the precise nature of your relationship, I think it's better for all parties if you stay away from him."

"Mom?"

That was Adam's voice. It was followed by his head peeking around the corner into the hallway.

"Freddy? Everything okay?" His brow furrowed.

Freddy wanted to smooth it with his fingers. With his mouth. But he couldn't, so he did the next best thing, and said, "Yes. Everything's okay."

And it was, he assured himself. He'd made a misstep, by coming here. They'd go back to the way things were, walking, talking, fucking in their own little bubble. For now.

And somehow, they'd figure out another way.

They'd have to, because he already knew that as much as he loved Adam, the bubble wasn't going to be enough, not indefinitely.

Present day

And so Adam found himself in the Hamptons. He and Rusty were staying in the pool house of one Mr. Harry Smith—who had, somewhat to Adam's surprise, turned out to be an actual person.

"How are you both doing crammed in there?" Harry was serving glasses of rosé by the pool, as he often did in the evenings. He was newly retired from a career managing high-end restaurants and professed to need something to do with himself—hence the daily poolside happy hours. It was no hardship for Adam, though, because he genuinely enjoyed Harry's company. In the week they'd been in town, he had spent most of his days reading and walking—and avoiding his mother and sister as much as possible—but he'd come to enjoy hanging out with Rusty and Harry for a while before the two of them headed out for dinner, either in nearby East Hampton or in one of the other towns in the area. Harry was well connected and seemed to have made it his mission to show Rusty a good time. He'd gotten Rusty a twice-weekly residency at a drag night that was decidedly more upscale than Whine, so Lady Merlot was enjoying herself, too.

"I'm sorry the pool house is so tiny. Remember there's always the guest room in the main house if one of you would like to move in there."

Was it Adam's imagination or did Harry kind of...smolder at Rusty when he said that?

As far as he could tell, Harry and Rusty had had some kind of summer fling in their youth and had recently reconnected through Facebook. The official story was that they'd met when Harry, who seemed to come from money, had vacationed near Bishop's Glen with his family. Beyond that, Adam could extract no details—which was weird. Usually Rusty was more than forthcoming about his present and past adventures, be they sexual or otherwise. He was a natural storyteller. But his lips were sealed, apparently, when it came to Harry. Regardless, whatever was in their past, they had fallen into an easy camaraderie.

The pool house was a two-bedroom retreat fifty yards or so from the main house. Despite Harry's apologies for its being small, Adam was delighted with the arrangement, not least because it meant he didn't have to stay with his mom and Betsy, who were currently staying at a house in Amagansett— the next town over—that was way too big and no doubt too expensive. He had been worried about them overstaying their welcome at Charlie's. On the one hand, he was relieved that hadn't happened, but on the other, how were they possibly paying for their new place?

Determined to find out, he invited them over for drinks one evening after Rusty and Harry had headed out. He had hoped one good thing that might come from the foreclosure would be that it wouldn't be his job anymore to worry about the family finances. Apparently, he'd been wrong.

"Well." His mother swept into the small pool house and

surveyed the open-concept living area with her eyes only—her head stayed perfectly still. "Isn't this...cute?" Wilhelmina had a way of using words to convey the opposite of their actual meaning.

"It's hardly bigger than your trailer, Adam!" Betsy teased.

"It's actually quite a bit bigger." The "trailer" was also not a trailer: an RV and a trailer were not the same thing. But why was he bothering? They had a limited capacity to see reason, and he needed to focus on the task at hand.

He let them talk for a while he made martinis. The topic du jour was Gwyneth Paltrow. Despite his mother's tendency toward fickleness, Gwyneth had been an evergreen topic since Adam had arrived. She apparently owned the house "seventeen doors down" from their place, and they were obsessed with the idea of running into her. They had lately moved on to debating the wisdom of just marching up and ringing her doorbell. They were neighbors, after all. The problem was her place was so well contained, they had no way of knowing if she was even in town, much less any way to actually reach the doorbell.

"I ordered the these amazing biofrequency stickers from goop." Betsy rolled up her sleeve to reveal some stickers with weird symbols on them affixed to her upper arm. "I can already feel the healing happening."

"Hasn't all that stuff been debunked?" Adam asked. "Like, by NASA?"

His sister just rolled her eyes at him.

All right. He could only take so much. He had a new Julian Fellowes waiting, and the sooner he did this, the sooner they'd leave. He'd taken to curling up with a book by the pool in the evenings. It wasn't the lake at Kellynch, but it was nice. So, in the name of moving things along, he came right out with it. "How are you affording the place you're renting?"

He'd shocked them. They both blinked rapidly.

His mother recovered first. "Adam, I'm sure that's not relevant to—"

"It is, though. It is relevant. You don't have any money."

His mother sucked in a breath, apparently gobsmacked that he would utter such a thing. Her surprise was probably justified, because he hadn't, historically, been this blunt with her. But how had that worked out for everyone?

"You're bankrupt," he added, just to make sure she understood him. Hell, if he was going there, he might as well *go there*.

"Adam!" she scolded.

"What? It's the truth. You have no source of income that I can tell. You blew through everything Dad left. You ran Kellynch into the ground. How are you affording a place in the Hamptons? How are you affording anything?"

His mother glanced at Betsy, whose eyes were wide.

"If you must know, we're housesitting." Betsy whispered the last word like it was a dirty one, like she was confessing to a heinous crime.

"Oh!" Adam was honestly shocked. That was actually a huge relief. He'd been picturing tens of thousands—hundreds of thousands—going on credit cards, since no bank worth its salt would extend his mother any additional credit. "How did you manage to get a housesitting gig...seventeen doors down from Gwyneth Paltrow?" His relatives were wily, but he wouldn't have thought them well connected enough, at least in this rarified social scene, to stumble into a situation like that.

"Our friend arranged it." His mother's words were short

and clipped as she glared at Betsy. She clearly hadn't wanted Betsy to spill the beans about their housing situation. "He's very well connected."

"What friend?" he asked. "Charlie?"

"Oh! Mom!" Betsy cried.

"I told you not to call me that here."

"Right. Sorry. Wilhelmina."

Adam raised his eyebrows questioningly.

"People think we're sisters," his mother said haughtily. "I see no reason to call their attention to the fact that that's not the case."

He chuckled. That was so her. It softened him a little, too, for some reason. "Look. I'm not trying to be a pain. I just don't want you to get into any trouble."

"Wilhelmina!" Betsy said urgently, before his mother could respond.

"Yes? What is it?"

"I've had the most delicious idea. We should introduce Adam to William Ellison."

The notion was clearly new to his mother. She furrowed her brow, but then, slowly, she seemed to warm to the idea. Her face softened, and she cocked her head. "You know, I think we *should*." She turned to Adam, and he physically recoiled a little. He knew that look. His mother could be as stubborn as Rusty when she wanted to. It was just that Adam was not usually the focus of her machinations. She would offhandedly criticize his appearance, but she usually didn't bother with actual scheming when it came to him.

"The friend who set us up with the housesit is William Ellison," she said. "He owns a vineyard on the North Fork— isn't that the funniest coincidence? We met at a party Charlie took us to shortly after we arrived, and of course you can imagine that when he learned we were both winemakers, we became fast friends. We've had so many long chats about winemaking."

Adam didn't point out that Dad had been the actual wine-maker and that she had never taken any particular interest in the process except to the extent that it yielded the wine she liked to drink and the money she liked to spend.

"He's down here quite a bit because he acts as his vine-yard's distributor and sales director. He has friends who are in Europe for the summer, so he arranged for us to housesit until Labor Day."

"He's much better connected than Charlie is," Betsy said. "He knows *everyone*."

"Even *Gwyneth*?" Adam couldn't help asking.

"Oh, shut up," Betsy said.

"So this guy William set you up with this housesitting gig," he said. That didn't seem unreasonable. Of course, what Adam wanted was for his family to face reality. Which meant getting jobs. But since that didn't seem like it was going to happen anytime this century, a free place to stay wasn't the worst thing in the world.

"He did," Betsy confirmed. "And the place seemed ever so much more suitable to us, given our sensibilities, than Char-lie's was. We had to *share* the guest room at Charlie's."

And of course, Charlie didn't have Gwyneth seventeen doors down the street. "Well, you can hardly be expected to stand for that."

"Right?" Betsy had missed his sarcasm.

His mother had been tapping her fingernails—perfectly manicured, as ever—on the table and looking off into space. Suddenly, seeming to have decided something, she turned to him. "I would very much like to introduce you to our new friend. I'm going to see if he's free tomorrow evening. Will you join us?"

He was surprised that she'd asked, and so politely, too. Usually his mother simply *told* him what she expected from him. "Sure." Of course, he'd rather curl up with a book by the pool, but since part of his rationale for coming here had been to check up on his relatives, it couldn't hurt to meet their fairy godfather, the mysterious and well-connected William.

His mother's gaze slid down his jeans-and-T-shirt-clad body. "Wear something nice. Of course there's nothing to be done about those freckles on such short notice, but it wouldn't kill you to get a haircut."

Coming back to the restaurant was surreal. Freddy felt simultaneously like nothing had changed and everything had changed. The food was the same, the staff was the same, the customers were the same. Everything was the same.

So why did it all feel so different? Like he was skating along the surface of his life, correcting people's timing in the kitchen, placing the seafood order, filling in at the host stand when someone called in sick. It was *all the same*, he kept telling himself.

But if that was true, why did he feel like he could no longer fully immerse himself in this world he'd spent the last eight years building?

Maybe it was because Ben wasn't here? He'd left Ben in pretty good spirits in Bishop's Glen. He'd taken to visiting Lulu, of all people, every day. It had started with a visit to her in the hospital after the accident. Ben had felt responsible, since her injury had happened on his property. Whatever her faults, she'd seemed to have a cheering effect on Ben, one that Freddy hadn't managed to achieve in the weeks he'd spent there. When he'd broached the idea of returning to the city, they'd decided he would head back to the restaurant and Ben would follow within the next couple of weeks.

It was good that Ben had Lulu. For a while, Freddy thought maybe Ben and Adam would become friends, given their mutual interest in books. They'd certainly geeked out enough together at that dinner party. But Adam had left.

Just left without a word. To go to the Hamptons with Rusty, which Freddy only knew because he'd run into Adam's brother, Mark, visiting Lulu.

Not that he expected Adam to inform him of his comings and goings.

But still.

He knew why Adam had left. And why he—Freddy—was losing his mind so utterly.

It was that kiss. That astonishing, sweet-yet-hot kiss. The one that had threatened to completely undo him. The one that had scared the hell out of him.

The one Adam had called *epically stupid.*

"Hey, Chef!"

Freddy's thoughts were interrupted by Andie, a line cook who stepped in to act as expeditor when they were really slammed, which they were at the moment.

"Sorry. Yeah?" He shook his head. It was Saturday night, and he was supposed to be searing steaks.

"I've got two plates of mashed getting cold waiting for those." She nodded at the pair of raw steaks on the work surface in front of him.

Shit. Usually Andie barked orders from a perch in the center of the kitchen where she could see everything. The fact that she'd had to come over here to get his attention wasn't good. She wouldn't call him on it, though, since he was the boss.

"Right. Dump those mashed and start over. Tell the line cooks I'm sorry."

Sorry. He'd been saying that a lot lately. He laid the steaks on a hot cast-iron skillet.

He just couldn't seem to get back into the swing of things —couldn't break through the surface. He was antsy, too, hot all the time in the stifling kitchen. Unable to concentrate. His brain just wasn't moving fast enough. That damn town, with its fresh, green air and its endless starry skies, had infected him.

Well, the town and something else.

Some*one* else.

Someone, he reminded himself for the thousandth time, who hadn't even bothered to tell him he was leaving.

Someone who'd made it very clear, eight years ago, that he didn't want Freddy. And you couldn't undo eight years of heartache with one meaningless kiss.

CHAPTER THIRTEEN

Eight years ago

Freddy tried to regroup after the disastrous family dinner. The warm summer weather hanging on into September made it easier to slide back to the way things were, to walk and talk and kiss and swim and fuck. It was easy to be with Adam, he told himself, because that's what he'd always told himself.

Because it was *true*.

Or it had been true.

He *wanted* it to still be true, but nothing was the same after that dinner, after he'd truly seen what he was up against. It might be an unseasonably warm fall, but winter was coming all the same.

One night, a couple weeks later, Adam disappeared after they dried off, like he always did, leaving Freddy to dress alone by the lake.

When he reappeared, he was carrying a single pink flower. "Peony season is long gone, but the dahlias are blooming now. Don't you think they look kind of similar?" He held the flower out to Freddy, and Freddy's heart, a la the Grinch, grew almost uncomfortably large for his chest.

Freddy had idly admired a bush by the entrance to Kellynch once when he'd dropped Adam off here—back when they were still saying goodbye at the foot of the driveway. It had been positioned under a streetlight, so it had been easy to see that it was bursting with huge pink blossoms—peonies, apparently, though Freddy hadn't known that at the time. Adam had decided they were Freddy's favorite flower—and so they had become Freddy's favorite flower. He'd never had one of those before. After that first time he'd voiced admiration for the flowers, Adam had given him one at the end of every visit until they had stopped blooming.

"Thanks," he croaked, taking the flower with one hand and settling the other on Adam's waist and pulling him in for a kiss.

He was going to have to talk to Adam. To force things, eventually. It wasn't going to be easy.

But fuck easy. None of this was easy anymore. It *hurt* to have your chest forced open like this.

But he loved it. He needed it.

Impulsively, he slid his ring off, the one Adam always seemed to enjoy playing with when it was on Freddy's finger. "I want you to have this."

Adam's eyes widened. "You can't give me your ring."

"I can, though." This part *was* easy. That flower—what had he called it? A dahlia?—had made something bloom in his chest, something that was delicate like a flower but somehow also stronger than a flower. He wanted to make a reciprocal gesture. He wanted to bind them together so that when the storm came, they'd emerge from it together.

He didn't have flowers, or money, or anything, really. The

ring was the only object he owned that he truly gave a shit about.

The ring was sized for Freddy's middle finger, so it would be too big for all of Adam's, which was just as well because he didn't want Adam to interpret it as a proposal or anything. Well, in truth, he'd love it if Adam would interpret it as a proposal. He'd drop to one knee right here in the dirt if he thought he had any chance in hell of getting a yes. But they were a long way from that. All he could do was hope that someday, they'd get there.

"Don't freak out." He placed the ring in Adam's palm and closed Adam's fingers over it. "It's not a wedding ring or an engagement ring. It doesn't have to mean anything."

"But it does mean something." Adam's voice was thick with emotion. "Even if not that."

"Yeah. Yeah it does."

I hope.

Present day

"I've had the most astonishing text from Mark, by the way."

Adam's mother paced the living room of the luxurious housesitting pad, running her fingernails along a console table as she did so.

They were waiting for William Ellison, who, in the twenty-four hours since Adam had learned of his existence, had taken on almost legendary proportions. He was exceedingly well connected yet modest about those connections. Well-bred yet kind. He understood the importance of family. His taste was exquisite. He knew someone who knew Gwyneth.

He probably pooped rainbows.

"Oh?" Adam tried to think what news from Bishop's Glen could be considered astonishing and came up short. "What did Mark have to say?"

His mother paused her pacing and raised her eyebrows. "Ben Captain and Lulu McGuire are dating."

"*What?*"

Betsy's shriek was echoed by a silent one inside Adam's head. His mother might as well have announced that the apocalypse was scheduled for the next five minutes, so surely did his body enter fight or flight mode. He managed to make himself sound normal, though—he hoped—when he squeaked out a comment designed to get his mother to add more detail without making it seem like he was hanging on that detail. "That seems like an odd match."

"It does indeed." His mother wrinkled her nose. Like Mark and Chloe, she had a complicated relationship with the McGuires, both admiring and resenting their wealth.

But in a way, Adam could kind of see it. Lulu wasn't a scholar, but she was fun and vibrant, and Ben needed that right now. Ben was handsome and quietly charming. And of course Lulu would be attracted to his wealth. He just hoped she was attracted to more than that.

"I wonder how Freddy Wentworth is taking it." Bless his sister for verbalizing the question that had been vibrating on Adam's tongue. "Mark told me earlier that it sort of seemed like there might be something between Freddy and Lulu."

"Apparently fine," his mother answered. "Mark reports that Freddy was at the McGuires' saying goodbye to both of them—he headed back to the city a week ago, I gather—and everyone was smiling and Freddy and Ben seemed as close as ever."

Oh, God. Something unfamiliar began to unfurl in Adam's chest, slowly but decidedly. He was pretty sure that, even though he was unfamiliar with the sentiment, it was hope.

Which he should quash. Because, objectively speaking, there wasn't any. That ship had sailed. Freddy had rebuffed Adam's kiss the other day, and now he was back in New York City, where he belonged.

But it felt so good, this hope. It was warm and tingly and—

"What are you so happy about?" Betsy demanded.

"Whatever it is, wipe that idiotic grin off your face," his mother said. "I don't want William to think you're a simpleton."

"I'm sure it doesn't matter what William thinks of me," Adam said peevishly. He didn't *want* to wipe the idiotic grin off his face. It had to be done, of course—the hope inside him had to be extinguished. But he'd do it on his own schedule, his mother, his sister, and His Highness William, Prince of the Hamptons, be damned.

"Shh!" his mother hissed as someone knocked on the door. "And *try* not to limp too badly."

Then she waited. Stood still as a statue. Adam refrained from rolling his eyes, but only just. She always did this thing where she waited to answer the door because she didn't want to seem overeager. Adam was pretty sure the length of time she waited was proportional to how impressed she was by the person on the other side. William Ellison merited a full thirty seconds.

"William!" Adam's mother managed to infuse her voice with just a hint of surprise, as if she hadn't invited William— as if she hadn't literally been pacing the floor on the other side of the door anticipating his arrival. She ushered him in, said,

"I'm so pleased to introduce you to my son Adam," and Adam knew.

William was gay.

His mother had neglected to mention that.

Adam had never had particularly reliable gaydar—Henry McGuire, for example, had surprised him. But there was no mistaking the look William gave him as he drawled, "I've heard *so* much about you."

Adam was sure he had. The question was whether any of it was true.

William was older than Adam would have expected—his mother idealized youth, after all. Adam put him in his very late forties. He was tall and dark with a neatly trimmed beard that contained some silver. He wore loose ecru linen pants and a long-sleeved pale pink button-down shirt with the sleeves rolled to above his elbows. He was generically handsome. Adam had always thought there was beauty in imperfection— in a vine that had become gnarled as it refused to grow in the direction you wanted it to.

In Freddy's broken nose.

William had no imperfections to speak of. If there was such a thing as Hamptons Ken, William was it.

Suddenly, his mother and sister's cryptic scheming of last night made sense—they were aiming to fix him up with William. Which was weird. His mother, to her credit, didn't do that. Probably because Adam was generally beneath her notice, but he benefited from her inattention in that regard. He wondered what nefarious purpose she had in mind here.

Despite his unease, Adam did what was required of him. He always did, though honestly, he was beginning to question why. He shook hands—William held his just a beat too long— and smiled and offered to make William a drink.

William wasn't bad company. Adam felt a little guilty. What did it say about him how suspicious he automatically was of anyone who would associate with his family? But William turned out to be funny and good-natured. He seemed to have more of a handle on the reality of the situation than Adam would have expected. Once, when his mother and Betsy were carrying on about Gwyneth—when were they ever going to *see* her?—William caught Adam's eye and winked. Then he said, all solicitousness, "I'm sorry, ladies. My reach only extends so far. My wine doesn't make the cut at Gwyneth's parties."

Adam's mother made a dismissive gesture. "Your wine is wonderful. I'm sure Gwyneth simply hasn't had the chance to try it yet."

William shrugged. "I do what I can, but this is Long Island, not Provence." He aimed another wink at Adam, who found himself charmed by William's easy self-deprecation.

"When we meet Gwyneth," Betsy said, "we'll give her a bottle."

"You are too kind," William said.

The rest of the evening went like that, William displaying genuine and seemingly unconditional kindness to Adam's relatives and, at the same time, sharing conspiratorial glances with Adam. He and Adam spent a fair amount of time talking about wine. It was nice, even if it did make him think about how much he missed Kellynch. About what he had lost.

But all in all, Adam was surprised by how much he *liked* William.

And by how flattered he was to get a text from him the next morning.

I wondered if you'd like to join me for a
drink this evening.

Alone in his bedroom at Harry's pool house, he grinned. It wasn't that he was attracted to William. He was a little too perfect. A little too smooth and plastic: Middle-Aged Hamptons Ken. But still, it was invigorating to sought after by a man like that. To be asked out directly, with no dissembling.

He hesitated over his response. He was pretty sure he didn't want to go on a date-date with William. But as a thought experiment, he allowed himself to wonder what it would be like if he did. He had enjoyed the man's company last night. It wasn't like anything physical had to happen. And how about another thought experiment? What if something physical *did* happen? Would that be the end of the world? He was young, single, and on vacation.

And as much as he wished he could pretend otherwise, Freddy didn't want him.

He picked up his phone. His mother would counsel him not to answer right away so as not to seem overeager. Screw that.

Adam: I actually have plans to go see a
friend of mine who's performing tonight at
Blue Dolphin. Would you like to join me
there?

Though he'd gone to Rusty's first performance, Adam hadn't caught one since and had been planning to go tonight. And hanging out at a bar with something to distract them would make the evening seem less overtly date-like.

William: I would like that very much. Can I pick you up?

Adam thought about it for a second. No. That was too date-y.

Adam: I'll meet you there. Say ten?

William: Looking forward to it.

"I think your mother is trying to set us up," William said with another one of those conspiratorial smiles as soon as they'd sat down at the bar.

Adam was a little taken aback, but also a little charmed, by the forthrightness of this statement.

"I can't say I mind," William went on.

"The question is, what's in it for her?" Adam said, deciding to meet forthrightness with forthrightness.

"What do you mean?" William leaned in like he was genuinely interested in what Adam had to say.

"I mean my mother. Don't take this the wrong way. I love her. But her schemes are usually firmly self-serving."

William threw his head back and laughed. "And that is precisely why I like her. She doesn't pretend to be anything she's not."

"Don't let you hear her say that. I think she thinks she pretends rather well."

"Well, perhaps she's more transparent in her machinations than she intends," William agreed affably. He rested his chin on his hands. "Unlike you. You don't scheme at all, do you?"

Adam shrugged. "I don't really see the point of it."

"Which is exactly why I like *you* so much."

Adam felt a blush starting. Thankfully, the lights went down, and an emcee came onto the little stage to introduce Lady Merlot.

"This is your friend?" William leaned over to talk into Adam's ear. Was it Adam's imagination or did he linger there a beat longer than necessary?

Lady Merlot made eye contact as Adam nodded against William's face, which William still hadn't fully retracted. Lady Merlot's eyebrows shot up. Then she smiled. And even though she usually had a strict policy of not talking before her first song, she winked at Adam and said, "This first number goes out to all the lovebirds out there." Then, damn her, she launched into "Pink Cadillac," a song bursting with sexual innuendo, switching the pronouns and having "Adam" tempting "his sweetie" instead of the "Eve" of the original song.

Despite his embarrassment, Adam had fun. Mostly. At least until the set was over and Lady Merlot came out to join them and started getting all nosy.

"Delighted, I'm sure." Lady Merlot gave William her hand as Adam performed introductions. Then she and William proceeded to charm each other. It was a little odd. It was almost like they were both...performing. Adam was used to that from Rusty, of course, in his Lady Merlot persona, at least. And he didn't know William that well, but suddenly, watching him from afar, something about the nature of his attention to Lady Merlot seemed...off.

He shook off the sense of unease, though, as Lady Merlot said her goodbyes and headed backstage to change for the second set.

"Should we get out of here?" William said.

Adam nodded. "I'm beat." *Translation: time to go home. Alone.*

William took the hint. "Can I drive you?" He rested a hand against Adam's lower back as he propelled him through the crowd, which had thickened considerably since they arrived.

"I prefer to walk," Adam said. "I'm a big walker."

"Can I walk you?"

Something caught in Adam's chest to remember the other time a man had so effortlessly shifted gears from *Can I drive you?* to *Can I walk you?*

"I'm fine on my own." Adam smiled to show that the rejection wasn't personal. He really just wanted to breathe some fresh air, clear his head, listen to silence.

"All right," William said when they emerged onto the street. "Can I kiss you?" He grinned. "I'm guessing that's also no, but a guy can hope."

"You guessed right. But I do appreciate being asked." Both because it was flattering, and because most guys wouldn't have bothered asking. They would have just taken.

"Maybe next time?"

Adam smiled again. It *was* nice to be asked. "Maybe."

"Humor an old man and text me when you get home so I don't worry?"

"Will do." Adam turned and started for Harry's place.

It was a long walk. He actually wouldn't have minded company. A certain kind of company. A certain kind of company that, no matter how charming William had been, Adam couldn't get out of his mind.

CHAPTER FOURTEEN

Eight years ago

"You are insane."

Adam bristled under Rusty's assessment. It wasn't that he expected him to be all gung ho over the idea, but God, was it too much to expect his best friend to be a little more sympathetic?

"I have the security deposit and first month's rent and enough saved to buy furniture! I thought you *wanted* me to move out!"

"Adam." Rusty said his name like he was a kindergartener in need of reasoning with. Seated at the desk in the small office in the shop, he looked at the ceiling, as if appealing to the heavens for divine patience.

"It's just an apartment, Rusty. A one-year lease. I'm almost twenty. I don't need to be living at home anymore."

"That's right. You're almost twenty. You *shouldn't* be living at home. You should be far away, living in a tiny shoebox of a room with a roommate you hate, worried about your midterms."

Arg! Adam wanted to scream. "I don't know why you're so obsessed with the idea of me leaving town. *You* live here."

"Don't be like me."

Rusty, clearly as frustrated with the conversation as Adam was, rose, crossed the office, and poured himself a cup of coffee. Only when he'd doctored it to his specifications, did he turn back to Adam. He remained standing and said, "Is this about Freddy Wentworth?"

"No. This is about me."

"But also about Freddy Wentworth?"

The ring Adam wore on a chain around his neck suddenly felt like it weighed a thousand pounds. Like it was glowing ultraviolet. Like even though it was hidden under his shirt, there was no way for Rusty *not* to see it.

"Adam." Rusty's tone had gentled. "Please tell me. What is he to you? I can tell you've been hiding something from me."

He had been, though he wasn't sure why. They both knew the truth. Why not confirm it? It was nothing to be ashamed of.

"I'm in love with him."

Rusty nodded like he wasn't surprised, but it was a grim nod.

"And he's in love with me," Adam added, almost petulantly.

Rusty's nostrils flared. "Freddy Wentworth is in love with you."

"Is that so impossible to believe?"

"Adam." His name again—again like he was a kid who wouldn't listen. Adam hated being talked to like this. "If the love nest you're thinking of renting is the prison keeping you here, Freddy Wentworth is the jailor. He'll lock you in and throw away the key, and you'll never get out."

"I don't want to get out, Rusty. That's the thing." Adam sighed, defeated. He should never have asked for Rusty's blessing. "I *like* Bishop's Glen."

"Have I ever led you astray?" Rusty said suddenly.

"What?"

"In the years you've known me, what have I been to you?"

"You've been everything." That was true.

"I've given you a job. A place to live when you needed it."

"And you've been my friend," Adam added, because even though they were in the middle of a tiff, that was important. Rusty had been there for him when no one else had.

"Right. And with that comes advice, whether you like it or not."

Adam smiled. He didn't like it, in this particular case, but he did sort of like it in general. It felt good to have someone in your life who was so invested in your future that they got pissy with you.

Or at least it had historically.

"And you need to listen to me now, regardless of whether you get the apartment or not. I know you don't want to hear it, but age does bring wisdom. I understand that Freddy is fun. Maybe I should have been more accepting of this…affair. But it's not going to last. You can't plan your whole life around it. You're too young, for one thing. If it doesn't end in outright heartbreak, whatever has been between you is going to fade, just like summer. Because that's what happens. That initial rush goes away. And as hard as it is, you have to ask yourself, what am I going to be left with when it does?"

Wow. That was…quite the speech. "You don't understand," Adam tried to protest, but his voice sounded feeble, unconvincing, to his own ears. "He's different than—"

"Spare me. I know him."

"You *don't*, though."

"I know his type." Rusty blew out a breath and looked up to the ceiling for a moment. When he righted his head again, his face was different. Hard. Cold. Adam had never seen him like this.

"And now, my darling, it's time for some tough love. Yes, I want you to get the hell out of this town. Getting an apartment in Bishop's Glen is the first step in admitting that you are never going to *leave* Bishop's Glen. You know my sofa is always available to you if your mother gives you shit, but if you get your own place in this godforsaken town, you're fired —as both my employee and my friend."

Adam sucked a breath in and recoiled. Rusty might as well have slapped him.

"I'm sorry. I know this hurts, but it's for your own good." Rusty laid a hand on Adam's arm. "Someday, you'll understand that I was right about all of this."

Present day

Adam did let William kiss him next time they went out. They'd been to dinner at a restaurant his mother informed him had a three-month waiting list for people who weren't William Ellison.

Adam had allowed himself to be plied, basically, with food and wine and compliments.

He still wasn't precisely sure why his mother was so gung

ho on the match, except perhaps that at the end of the summer, when the housesit was up, she would need somewhere else to go. But it wasn't like Adam was going to marry William and move his crazy family in with him. Adam liked to watch *Masterpiece Theatre*, not live it. But maybe she was relying on William's connections for more free housing post–Labor Day and considered Adam a pawn in her scheming.

The kiss, which occurred by the pool at Harry's—Adam had allowed William to drive him home, too—had been a not-unpleasant diversion. Exactly the kind of kiss you'd expect from Hamptons Ken. In fact, Adam kind of felt like *he* was a Ken doll, too, like his body was covered with smooth, impenetrable, plastic flesh. Because the kiss had been an above-the-neck experience only.

In Adam's experience, there were two types of kisses. The first was the frantic, toothy kind he'd exchanged with random men in his few years of hooking up. Those had been previews of what was to come. And since he'd usually only hooked up when he was already super horny, he'd rushed through those kisses, had considered them rote preludes to what was to come.

And then there were the other kind of kisses: Freddy's. They'd been electric—the ones from eight years ago and the aborted attempt a few weeks ago. Both ends in and of themselves *and* previews. Both enough and not enough at the same time. Sometimes, he'd felt like he could kiss Freddy forever. And the feeling must have been mutual, because some nights, they'd spent *hours* kissing in the lake. Others, they'd been more hurried, overtaken by the arcs of electricity their mouths unleashed in each other. But even then, those kisses had been their own things—he never would have wanted to skip them.

William's kiss was neither of those things. It was…fine.

Maybe it would have had the potential to become more, if Adam hadn't gently pulled away and said, "I had a nice time tonight."

William rested his head against Adam's. "I did, too." He was breathing harder than Adam.

"I'm sorry," Adam said.

"You're sorry? Why?"

He took a step back, severing the connection between their foreheads. "I'm sorry I'm not..." This was awkward. "I'm old-fashioned, I guess," he finished feebly.

William shook his head gently. "Maybe. But maybe I like old-fashioned." He took Adam's hand, lifted it to his mouth, and kissed it.

It seemed like a line from a play. Like William was an actor saying the next line of dialogue in the script.

It was good dialogue, though. Adam watched him walk through the gate and into the night. This was probably the part where he was supposed to get butterflies in his stomach. Or twirl happily as he skipped off to bed. He ordered himself to feel...something.

"Well, if that wasn't the cutest thing I've ever seen."

"Ahh!" Adam jumped about a foot. "Rusty."

His friend's voice was coming from a dark corner of the yard. Adam moved toward it. Rusty, in his Lady Merlot persona, was stretched out on a lounge chair sipping a glass of wine. "Sorry, darling. I came out here to look at the stars, and I dozed off. By the time I woke up, I was stuck. I didn't want to interrupt you, so I sat here, quiet as a mouse and minded my own business."

Adam shook his head and sat on the foot of Rusty's chair. He should be angry. Or at least annoyed. But once again, he couldn't make himself feel much of anything.

"However," Rusty said, "I want you to know, I approve." He lifted his glass in a toasting gesture. "I approve *whole-heartedly*."

Adam sighed and looked at the stars. They were, objectively, beautiful. But they only made him long for the fake ones on the ceiling at home.

The *next* time Adam went out with William—which was something he kept doing because in addition to making his mother and Rusty happy, it was a not-unpleasant way to pass the time—he *definitely* felt something.

Because, after leaning in close to William to look at a series of pictures on his phone, he sat back, looked up, and saw Freddy.

Freddy.

Freddy who was sitting at the bar watching him, a killer scowl on his face.

And yep, there was all that missing sensation. It all poured into him at once, flooding his body with panic and joy at the same time. How could Freddy be *here*?

"Are you all right?" William laid a hand on top of Adam's. He felt it like a shackle, an unwanted staking of claim. He wanted to snatch his own hand away, but he was frozen. His entire body had stopped, turned inward to witness fear and hope unspooling in equal measure. The only parts that seemed to function were his eyeballs, which he darted once again to where Freddy was sitting.

He was pushing back from the bar. *Oh, my God.* Was he coming over here? Adam had to get his hand back from William.

But no. Freddy merely threw some money on the bar, turned without making further eye contact, and left.

Adam did take his hand back then, but it was too late.

Freddy pushed out of the restaurant, which was owned by an acquaintance, and took big, gulping lungfuls of air. What the fuck was he doing here? Here at this bar and, more generally, here in the Hamptons. Either. Both.

He'd been prepared—he thought—to see Adam. That was *why* he'd come, after all. He could tell himself all kinds of stories about this being an exploratory trip. About having decided he was sick of New York City and maybe interested in opening a place somewhere quieter.

But if that was the case, why hadn't he talked to Ben about it? They had speculated casually, over the years, about opening a second place. Ben would have been all over the idea of a Captain's Hamptons outpost—this was a much more logical place for a seafood restaurant than New York City. Hell, he'd probably try to talk him into something in the Finger Lakes so he could be closer to his house there. Ben had never taken to the city like Freddy had.

Or like Freddy *thought* he had.

He thought he'd become a true New Yorker, hard and impenetrable. That he was immune to things like nature and quiet and…love. Now, going through his routine in the city, walking from his apartment to the restaurant, dividing his day between the executive part of his executive chef title and the actual chefing he preferred, he tried to lose himself in the dinner rush each evening, finishing the night with more whiskey than was probably advisable.

He kept telling himself it was the same as it had always been. It was all what he'd professed to be missing the whole time he was in Bishop's Glen.

Yet none of it was the same. And, more astonishingly, he *hated* it. That initial sense that he didn't fit into his life anymore had deepened, taken on an edge. It had become bad enough that he'd started playing hooky. Calling in sick to the restaurant. Calling in sick to his own life—the one he'd made for himself, presumably to his own specifications. He just couldn't face day after day of cooking for well-heeled New Yorkers anymore.

So he'd come on this fool's errand, letting his battered heart lead the way for once. He'd wanted to see Adam—it was as simple as that. He wasn't sure what that would accomplish precisely, just that he thought he might feel better if he did.

The thing was, he hadn't been prepared to see Adam *right then*. He'd just gotten to town. Had been planning to chat up the bartender and leverage some restaurant connections, ask around and find out if anyone knew anything about any of the Elliots—either his Elliot or the nutbar wing of the family—or about a socket-wrench-wielding, wine-swilling drag queen, for that matter. He was ready to play detective.

And yes, maybe gather some intel about the local restaurant scene—so he could at least pretend there had been a larger purpose for this trip.

He was *not* ready to have the mystery solved by running smack dab into Adam getting all cozy at an intimate table for two with some man who was old enough to be his father.

God. Why did he keep *doing* this? When was he ever going to learn?

CHAPTER FIFTEEN

Eight years ago

"It's too cold to swim," Adam said as he and Freddy turned up the drive to Kellynch in late September. Normally, he loved the fall. By mid-October the property would be edged with sugar maples that had turned a brilliant red, and the smell of decaying leaves would swirl together with the ever-present pine scent of the surrounding forests to fill his head with the smell of home.

This year, he hated the fall. Dreaded October.

They'd taken to hanging out in the barrel room, which was in an outbuilding. When they were outside, and swimming, everything had been magical. Adam had been sharing his beloved Kellynch with his beloved Freddy. Now, as they sat with a flashlight among rows of barrels full of wine at varying points in the fermentation process, it felt like hiding. And the barrel room at Kellynch, unlike at some of the other wineries in the region, was utilitarian. Since they had never done tours, it was chilly and bleak, and there was nowhere to sit except on the concrete floor.

And the deeper they'd gotten into fall the less...patient Freddy seemed. Oh, he was still the same old kind, chivalrous Freddy, but he'd started talking about stuff that usually didn't intrude on their time together. He kept asking questions about Rusty. About Adam's time living with Rusty when his family had kicked him out. He kept talking about wanting to go out to dinner. He'd even invited Adam to the town's annual grape stomp—Adam, of course, had had to decline because his family would be there representing Kellynch Estates.

When they got to their usual spot behind a rack of barrels, Adam sat. He was distracted by arranging his legs, so he didn't notice at first that Freddy hadn't joined him. He shined his flashlight up, not into Freddy's face because he didn't want to blind him, but at his chest. Ambient light from the beam illuminated his face, usually so familiar and dear to Adam, in such a way that he looked...not himself. Shadows did funny things to his eyes—they disappeared into their sockets. Adam shivered.

"I can't keep doing this," Freddy whispered.

No. Adam's stomach dropped. The taste of metal flooded his mouth. But he'd known, in his heart, that this was coming. Things hadn't been the same between them lately. Yes, they were doing the same things—the walking, the swimming, but they were the same only on the surface.

Before, there hadn't been any difference, with Freddy and him, between what was on the surface and what was on the inside. That was the amazing thing about Freddy. Adam could show him his true self, and Freddy reciprocated. It was simple, but it was revolutionary.

"Are you breaking up with me?" He hated how pitiful his voice sounded, but it did a pretty good job communicating the misery in his heart.

"No." Any relief Adam felt was short-lived when Freddy added, "I'm asking you to make a choice." Freddy did sit then, leaning against the wall and taking Adam's hand as Adam struggled to breathe. He spoke extremely gently. "What I mean is I'm tired of all this sneaking around. Why are we hiding? We're both out."

"It's complicated. The thing with my family is—"

"I get that. I really do. But in some ways, it's *not* complicated. It's getting cold. What are we going to do when winter really hits? Build an igloo?"

Adam couldn't really argue with that, even if he had been able to breathe.

"It's not just that," Freddy went on. "I want you to make as much noise as you want to when I blow you. I want blow you under the blinding sun of high noon."

Despite the cold, Adam's cheeks heated.

"Hell, I want to go stomp on some fucking grapes with you under the blinding sun of high noon—that's how far gone I am over you. Remember that time we got coffee after I brought my car to the garage?"

He did. That day had marked the beginning of Rusty's suspicions regarding Freddy.

"Or that time you delivered my car and we grabbed dinner? I want to do that again. Without an excuse."

"I thought about moving out," Adam said quietly. "About getting an apartment."

"You did?" They only had the dim illumination of the flashlight, but Adam could tell that Freddy's face had lit up.

He was surprised, in addition to delighted, which stung a little. But it shouldn't have, because what Adam was going to say next would be a return to form in Freddy's eyes. "I decided I can't afford it."

"Financially?" Smart Freddy knew there were so many layers here.

"Partially," Adam whispered.

If he moved out, he'd lose his job and hence his income. But he would also lose his family and, more important, his only real friend in this town. His only, and long-trusted, safety net. And since his big confrontation with Rusty, a little voice inside Adam had been asking *What if he's right?* Adam didn't have any experience with relationships, but everything he'd heard or read suggested that they *did* cool off over time. Did he really want to risk everything—give up everything—for Freddy so early in their relationship?

The way Freddy's face had crumpled told Adam that he understood what Adam had meant when he said, "Partially."

"Look." Freddy heaved a sigh and met Adam's gaze. "I didn't think I would ever say this, because you know how much I love you. I always thought I would do anything for you. Walk miles out of my way. Stop smoking. Arrange the world however you like it." He pulled his hand from Adam's grasp, and if Adam had felt earlier like he couldn't breathe, now it was like thousands of tiny needles were piercing his deflated lungs.

"But I can't anymore." Freddy's voice cracked, and so did Adam's heart, joining the carnage in his chest. "So you have to choose. Me or them."

"Them?" Adam wasn't sure why he was asking. He knew what Freddy meant.

"Your family. Rusty." He shrugged. "I don't know exactly.

Whoever has you so afraid to live your life the way you want to. The people you're hiding me from."

Hiding. Adam gasped, and something sharp and cold sliced through him. The truth had a way of doing that. "Why can't we just figure out a way through the winter?" he pleaded. If he just had some more time, he could be sure this was real. That it would last. That it was worth risking everything for. "And then next summer, I can—"

Freddy silenced Adam by holding up a hand. "I don't have much. I know that. I don't have money. I don't have an education. I know what people say about me." His voice wavered as he spoke. He paused and swallowed, and it sounded stronger when he continued. "The one thing I do have, have always had, is pride."

Adam knew what was coming, and he couldn't stop a tear from falling. Then another.

Freddy smiled sadly and cradled Adam's cheeks in his hands, using his thumbs to brush away his tears. "I would give up anything for you—except that." Then Freddy took his hands off Adam's cheeks, and Adam wanted to wail. He was being un-claimed. "I won't keep doing this. If you want me, we're not hiding anymore. I understand that might cost you, and I'll help you bear that cost. It's also possible that it won't be as bad as you think, that they'll come around. Regardless, I'm not spending the winter huddling in this barrel room. So, choose."

That last sentence was tinged with a harshness he'd never heard from Freddy.

The thing was, Adam knew his family wouldn't come around like they had last time, with his sexuality. And Rusty. Rusty didn't "come around."

"I'm sorry," Adam said, trying to make his voice sound

clear, even, to prevent the fear that was behind this decision from coming through. He should at least own his shame. He reached inside his shirt and pulled out Freddy's ring. He worked the chain over his head and removed the ring from it.

Freddy must have known what he intended, because he shook his head. "I don't want it back."

"I can't just keep it. You made this."

"I made it for you."

"You didn't even *know* me when you made it."

Freddy shrugged, like that was a minor detail. Like the reality of time and space didn't apply to them.

Hadn't applied to them—past tense.

"You can break up with me," Freddy said, "But you can't make me take that ring back."

And, then, chivalrous to the end, Freddy leaned over and kissed Adam on the cheek, got up, and left.

Present day

"It's not the whole symphony, Mother." Adam tried not to visibly roll his eyes. "The entire New York Philharmonic isn't going to come up here."

"It's merely a chamber ensemble," William said smoothly, pulling his car—he was driving all three Elliots to the concert —up to a gated compound and rolling down the window to speak to a man in the guardhouse.

"That's a subset of the whole orchestra," Adam translated, knowing that *chamber ensemble* wasn't something that would have any meaning to his mother and sister despite their aspirations. He twisted around to find her glaring at him. She'd insisted he sit up front with William, doing an embarrassing amount of theatrical wink-winking as the foursome prepared to depart.

She huffed at him. She hated being called out on lack of rich-people knowledge, but Adam figured it was better—for both of them—than if she embarrassed herself later.

"This place is certainly grand enough to house the entire New York Philharmonic," William said placatingly, pulling ahead after having received clearance from the guard.

"Do you think Gwyneth will be here?" Betsy asked.

"I'm afraid not," William said. "I've heard from a friend in the catering business that she's not in town."

Betsy pouted.

How had Adam ended up here? How was this his life?

They left the car with a valet, the irony of which was not lost on Adam.

The long path to the main house was lined with lanterns made from paper bags with candles in them, and as they started out on foot, William put his hand on Adam's lower back. He'd been doing that more and more lately. It was awkward. Adam didn't want it there, but unlike if William had tried to take his hand, he couldn't avoid it. The only way to escape was to walk faster than William, and Adam, though he loved walking, wasn't physically capable of that. So he was stuck.

He wondered if William had considered that.

He assumed not, because otherwise he wouldn't be doing it.

Or maybe he would. After all, the world was not exactly teeming with kind, considerate men who made the comfort of others a priority.

In other words, there was only one Freddy.

"Freddy! You came!"

Bronwen Worthington-Ware air-kissed Freddy as he made his way into an enormous ballroom-type space in her house.

Bronwen and her husband were regulars at the restaurant back in the city, and when she'd heard Freddy was in the Hamptons, she'd been generous with invitations and introductions.

He'd been using her, in truth. He'd told her this was a research trip, that he was thinking of opening a place here. He figured that by saying that, it might become true. That he could somehow make his trip here about that and not about Adam. As long as he did stuff—other stuff—he could justify his continued presence in the Hamptons.

So he was careful to ask Bronwen lots of questions about things like which restaurants in the area had been most enduringly successful. Did she think there was room for another seafood-heavy place, or should they branch out into something else?

She had embraced his phantom project with enthusiasm, meeting him to dine at various spots, introducing him to friends, and inviting him to her house.

"I have to run off to make sure the musicians have everything they need," she said, "but after the performance, I want to introduce you to a few people. There's a winemaker here from the island—William Ellison." She wrinkled her nose a little. "Probably you'd only be interested in his stuff for the lower end of your list, or if you want to do a cutesy, downmarket, all-local list, but it can't hurt to meet him." She grabbed a glass of champagne from a passing server and handed it to him. "Enjoy the music!"

He made his way deeper into the space, deflecting a seemingly endless parade of appetizers from passing waiters. Caviar and crème fraîche on toasted rye, lobster salad on endive, bacon-wrapped filet mignon bites. It was probably all delicious. Locally sourced and impeccably pedigreed.

It just made him tired.

The room was full of shiny people. They were sleek and polished and rich. They gathered in small clusters, mindlessly tossing back booze and those perfect canapés. Sometimes one of them threw a head back and laughed uproariously. It was like watching a nature documentary.

He didn't belong here.

And it wasn't because of his modest background. It wasn't the same feeling he'd always had as a kid in Bishop's Glen that his poverty or his lack of a father or his rough edges made him an outsider.

No, it was more that he didn't *like* these people. Which probably wasn't fair. Individually, many of them were no doubt fine. Bronwen, for instance, was friendly and insightful, and he enjoyed her company. And even collectively, these were the kind of people who ate at Captain's. If he'd been serious about opening a second place here, these *exact* people would be his customers. And because chefs—especially celebrity chefs—commanded a certain amount of respect, they would welcome him into their lives.

He just suddenly...wasn't interested in them. In feeding them or being one of them.

Or talking to them. So he took a seat near the back and on an aisle that ran along a side wall. Maybe some high culture would chill him out a little. Though this kind of music was more something Adam would enjoy. Freddy would take the Rolling Stones over chamber music any day. But as with

Adam's costume dramas, Freddy suspected that if he kept an open mind, he'd probably enjoy the concert more than he might expect.

"Fancy meeting you here."

The voice had come from behind him. He whirled.

As he did so, Adam, who'd sunk into the row behind him did a weird sort of ducking move. "I'm trying to hide." He twisted a little more. It was like he was trying to keep Freddy's body between him and the crowd.

Freddy allowed himself to be used thusly as he scanned the room. He caught sight of Wilhelmina and Betsy standing near the edge of a clump of people, one of whom he recognized as a minor Hollywood starlet.

He wasn't sure how he felt about Adam right at the moment. He was mad at him, he supposed, but that wasn't really fair. Adam didn't owe him anything—anymore. But as he watched Wilhelmina throw her head back and laugh, he did find himself sort of sympathetic to Adam's plight. His mother was mimicking the people around her, but if this had been a nature documentary, the narrator would be talking about how she was on the outskirts of the pack, lodged at the bottom of the pecking order but doggedly trying to make her way up.

Like Freddy, she didn't fit. Unlike him, though, she was trying to. It was painful to watch.

He sighed. Turned back to Adam but kept his torso angled so as to shield him as much as possible. He tried not to stare at Adam's lips. Tried not to think about the kiss they'd shared last time they were together—the kiss that had almost caused him to throw himself at Adam's feet and beg for another chance. "I was just thinking that this was more your scene than mine."

Adam's face lit up, and fuck if it wasn't like a lance directly to Freddy's heart. "You were?"

"If you rewound a couple centuries, this would look like a scene from that miniseries you used to watch."

"*Pride and Prejudice?*"

"That's the one with the hot guy in the old-fashioned shirt coming out of the lake?"

Adam grinned. "That's the one."

"Yep."

A waiter came by. Damn these servers. While on paper, Freddy could appreciate that they were actually doing a very good job—making sure that the food circulated widely, even as far as the people hiding in a corner in the back—he just wanted to be left alone. But maybe Adam wanted something to eat.

"Blue cheese and pear tartlets," the server murmured, and Freddy shifted so Adam could reach the plate.

"No thank you." Adam shook his head and smiled politely. When the server left, he said, "You know what I would really like instead of blue cheese and pears?"

"What?"

"Cheddar and apple. In grilled-cheese format. With that mayo thing. That was the best."

Yes. That was what Freddy wanted, too. Well, it was one thing Freddy wanted. Simple, good, unfussy food. His stomach rumbled at the thought.

"This fancy stuff is fine." Adam echoed Freddy's very thoughts. "But it gets tiresome." He flashed a self-deprecating grin. "Though I probably shouldn't say that to a chef."

"No. I know what you mean. Sometimes you want to just pare things down to the basics. What's good. What works."

Adam didn't answer right away. Just stared at Freddy in a way that made him want to squirm. "Yes," he finally said. Then he looked at the floor and did his signature blushing thing.

Goddamn it.

Freddy didn't even know what was going on, but he was pretty sure it deserved a *goddamn it*.

He cleared his throat. "I came up here because I'm thinking of opening a second place."

Which was a lie. It always had been, and his time here had confirmed that it always would be. He didn't want to open an outpost in the Hamptons.

"That's great!" There was genuine excitement in Adam's tone.

Freddy felt bad for lying, but he needed to explain his presence beyond *I came here to brood over you in person*. His pride demanded it.

"I'm sure it will be amazing." Adam smiled warmly. "I wish I could come back when it's open."

Aww fuck. That kind of unwavering confidence, bordering on hero worship? He didn't have any defenses against that, not when it came from Adam. "So you're not...staying here?"

Adam's good cheer disappeared. He sighed. "No. I'm just here checking up on my mom and sister."

Freddy followed Adam's gaze—back to the nature documentary. Wilhelmina and Betsy were still standing near the edge of the same clump of people, smiling with artificial brightness. "And how are they?"

"They are..." Adam huffed a laugh. Freddy couldn't tell if it was incredulous or bitter. "They are exactly the same, actually." Incredulous. Adam's voice had risen as he'd spoken, as if he were just coming to his conclusion and it surprised him. "They're probably oohing and aahing over those blue-cheese–pear things."

"There's actually a really fantastic fish-and-chips spot on the water," Freddy said. "Just a bit north of here."

But wait. What was he doing? Was he asking Adam out? He couldn't do that.

No, he was just letting Adam know. If Adam was pining for grilled cheese and turning his nose up at the stuff here, he would love the unassuming little mom-and-pop place that did the best double-fried chips, which, doused in vinegar, were smuttily spectacular. "I've only been here four days, but I've been up there twice. I dream about those fish and chips, basically." He grinned and gestured around the room. "They're the antidote to all this bullshit."

"That sounds amazing," Adam said. "One of the annoying things about my time here is that I've barely seen the ocean. Rusty and I are staying at a place with a pool, which is fine, but isn't the ocean the whole point of the Hamptons?"

Something unexpectedly light bubbled up in Freddy's chest, which had of late been so tight, so constricted. Well, fuck it. This was why Freddy had come, right? As ill-advised as it was. He'd come running up here, chasing some vague sense that just being around Adam, even if nothing ever got settled between them, would be better than staying in his half life in the city. And even all these years later—all this *pain* later—it was hard for him to hear Adam state a wish he had the power to grant and not make it happen. "This is going to sound crazy because it's a bit of a drive, but do you want to bust out of here and—"

"There you are."

It was the man who'd been with Adam the other night, the older man. He looked like a cross between an aging hippie and a record company mogul. Like he was trying hard to look young—but also trying hard not to look like he was trying.

He didn't sit down. Just stood behind Adam's chair. Put his hand in the middle of Adam's upper back.

Freddy wanted to hit him. To grab that arm and throw it away like a rotten piece of fruit. He wanted to fucking pummel him, actually.

But he wanted a lot of things he couldn't have. What else was new?

Adam was still looking at him expectantly, like he was waiting for Freddy to finish his question. He was sitting there, with another man's hand on his back, expecting Freddy to finish asking him out?

Yeah. Not happening.

Freddy might be kind of fucked in the head when it came to Adam Elliot, but he wasn't a *complete* idiot.

And really, this overgrown poseur asshole was doing him a favor. Reminding him to have some goddamn pride.

So he gazed back evenly at Adam, trying to make his mind and his face go blank.

The silence stretched on long enough that Adam's old-ass man-friend stuck out his hand and said, "I'm William Ellison."

Freddy blinked, startled. This was the winemaker Bronwen had planned to introduce him to. "Freddy Wentworth," he said.

William's eyes widened. "Of Captain's in Manhattan?"

"That's me."

"I'm a winemaker. I own Greenport Vineyards. Up in the North Fork."

Freddy made a noncommittal noise.

"Can I give you a card? Invite you up for a—"

"No." Freddy didn't care that he was interrupting. Being rude. "No, you cannot."

And with one more look at Adam—one he feared was not as neutral as he wanted it to be—he got up and left.

CHAPTER SIXTEEN

Eight years ago

Adam had a lot of experience with awkwardness. Trying to keep up when he was in a group on foot. Being anywhere in public with his mother or sister.

So he would have thought he'd be used to it. It turned out, though, that none of that had prepared him for what it felt like to make the biggest mistake of his life and then have to keep existing in the world like he was a normal person. Like he wasn't walking around with his mangled heart half inside his chest, half out as it tried to break free and go after the only thing it had ever really wanted.

The worst part was the ring. He'd given back to Freddy, and when Freddy had refused it, Adam had stuck it in his pocket. And, after Freddy had left, he'd laid on his back on the floor and cried. It had only been later that night, in his bedroom, that he'd realized it was missing. He'd gone back to the barrel room, of course, but it had been nowhere to be found. How could something like that just disappear? He'd wondered if maybe Freddy had come back for it after all. It seemed the only logical explanation.

Anyway, what did it matter? It wasn't like it was really his, despite Freddy's interpretation of things. He couldn't have kept wearing it. If he still had it, it would be hidden in one of his dresser drawers right now, out of sight but tormenting him just the same.

Still. He wanted it.

Sometimes people talked about heartbreak making them feel like they were missing a limb. That missing ring felt like a bigger deal than a missing limb—and Adam knew crappy limbs. He kept lifting his hand to stroke the ring—a mindless habit he had developed in the few weeks he'd worn it. Every single time he was surprised to find it was missing. Gutted anew.

"What's the matter with you?" Rusty asked. They were sitting on his sofa having a beer. Adam hadn't felt like going home after the shop closed, and Lady Merlot didn't have a gig tonight.

What if I just told him the truth? Not little half truths designed to test the waters. Not *I thought I might get an apartment,* but the actual truth.

"I made a huge mistake." He blew out a breath. It felt kind of amazing to say it out loud. So he kept going. "I was in love with Freddy Wentworth, and I dumped him. Now he's gone, and I feel like I'm going to die."

That felt even better. Well, not better. He still felt like crap. But speaking the truth in a direct way—like Freddy had always done—was surprisingly liberating.

"Don't be so dramatic, darling," Rusty said. "You got your heart a little banged up. Welcome to the human condition."

"What if I had left Bishop's Glen, like you always wanted?"

Adam asked, turning to his mentor, his friend, the man he was always trying to please. "What if Freddy and I had left together?"

Rusty rolled his eyes. "What does it matter? Freddy's gone."

It was true. It had been a month. Adam had tried to text him, to apologize, to take everything back, but there had been no answer. No indication that his texts had even been read. He'd asked around at Miller's, and all anyone knew was that Freddy had left suddenly, as had his friend Ben, and that he hadn't bothered to give notice.

"But just say things had gone differently. What if Freddy and I had moved somewhere…else? Somewhere bigger." *Somewhere we could really be together.* "New York City, maybe. I could have gone to school like you always wanted. Freddy could have…"

Rusty snorted. "What? What could Freddy have done? Washed dishes in New York? Where the cost of living is ten times what it is here?"

Adam didn't want to leave Bishop's Glen. He didn't want to leave Kellynch, but he knew then that he would have, if it would have let him be with Freddy. If it would have gotten him away from all these people who thought they knew how he should live his life.

He knew then that he *should* have.

Present day

```
Hey. Check this out.
```

The text from Sophie was accompanied by a photo of the waterfront at Kellynch. Freddy's breath caught. He switched on a bedside lamp in his hotel room—he'd been drinking and brooding in the dark since he got home from the concert—and enlarged the photo.

They'd cleaned up the little beach—installed a paved walkway that led to a new, much longer and sturdier dock, cleared the rocks and brush away and done some planting. It was made-over but still recognizable.

Still the place he'd left his heart.

There was a wooden structure on one end of the image, and what looked like small, high cocktail tables that people would stand at.

Freddy: Is that a bar?

Sophie: Yeah. We're going to cater in some wine and snacks for people while they're waiting for the boat. Kind of ironic that we live on a vineyard and have to bring wine in.

Freddy: It looks great.

It did. It was amazing what a little TLC could do.

Sophie: I also found this. I wonder if it belonged to one of the Elliots?

Freddy's stomach dropped when the picture came through. It was his ring. Dirty and looking a little worse for wear, but he'd recognize that mahogany band anywhere.

Fuck.

He had no idea what possessed him, after all these years, to tell her the truth. His fingers just did it.

```
Freddy: That's mine. I gave it to Adam
Elliot eight years ago because I was in love
with him.
```

Dropping the phone like it was contaminated, he threw his head back and laughed. It was kind of a maniacal laugh. It was late, and he was drunk. He hadn't been able to get the image of Adam, sitting calmly while William Ellison touched him, out of his head. He'd been seized with the notion that given all his past interest in winemaking, Adam had latched on to William. That maybe he hoped to find the love and approval from him that he'd never had from his father.

Or maybe it wasn't so complicated. Maybe Adam just *liked* William.

The prospect made him ill.

So he'd turned to whiskey, hoping it would dull the pain.

It had not.

The laugh might also have contained a little bit of genuine... Not happiness. Satisfaction. Telling the truth was liberating, in a way, even if it didn't elementally change anything.

The phone rang.

He could not answer, but he'd never get rid of her. She'd get in her car and drive here.

He picked up the call and instead of greeting her, he just sighed into the phone.

"What?" Her voice was low and almost shaky. Angry-sounding, actually. He'd expected shock, disbelief. He hadn't expected *pissed*. "What the *hell* are you talking about, Freddy?"

"I made that ring in high school. In shop class."

"I know," she snapped. "I remembered it the moment you said it was yours. You used to wear it. I guess I didn't notice when you stopped."

Silence settled for a moment. He knew there was no chance she'd leave it there, though.

And she didn't: "You know that's not what I meant when I asked you what the hell you were talking about."

Shit. He could hardly hold out on her. He was the one who'd brought this up.

"We met at Miller's." He flopped back on the bed and stared at the ceiling, which was spinning a little, thanks to his inebriation. "He was parking cars that summer before I left." She made a vague noise of dissatisfaction. Yeah, that wasn't what she wanted to know either. He sighed. "I don't know what else to tell you. I fell in love with him. I gave him that ring. It was good for a while."

It was her turn to be silent. He could picture her blinking, trying to adjust to the bomb he'd dropped. "And then what happened?" she finally said.

"Then it wasn't good." She didn't need to know all the gory details.

"And we took his house," she breathed, horror seeping into her tone.

"You didn't *take* it," Freddy corrected. "They lost it."

"Freddy, is this why you're in the Hamptons? Is *Adam Elliot* why you're in the Hamptons?"

He didn't answer. But he must not have needed to, because after a short stretch of silence, she asked, "What do you want me to do with the ring?"

"Nothing. Throw it away."

She laughed at him. He deserved it, probably, but it still rankled. "I'm not throwing it away."

"Do what you like with it, then. I don't want it." What the hell would he do with that ring, after all this time? He certainly couldn't wear it.

"I think you do want it. And I think you want Adam. I think you want Adam wearing it."

He did. The want she described was sharp and honed and polished, like a sword sliding in between his ribs. It hurt so much he sucked in a breath.

"Look," she said, her voice as gentle now as it had been angry at the start of the conversation. "I don't know what happened between you, but I know you. Don't cut off your nose to spite your face. Don't let this be like your hate-on for Bishop's Glen."

"I don't even know what that means." Why had he set himself up for this? *Why?*

"Yes, we had some shitty times here. But that's *life*. Life is shitty a lot of the time. If you have a chance to make it less shitty, don't let your stubbornness or your pride or whatever stand in the way."

Freddy reminded himself that his sister loved him. She meant well. But what she was instructing him to do was to give up everything. Every single thing he had. The qualities that had got him this far in life, propelled him out of Bishop's Glen and into a new life in New York.

A life he apparently didn't want anymore, judging by how long he'd lasted back there before retreating up here on his fool's errand.

So if, for one second, he entertained the notion that she might have been right, that maybe his stubborn pride *hadn't* always served him, he brushed it off. Because it didn't matter anyway. It wasn't up to him. There was already a hand resting on Adam Elliot's back, and it wasn't Freddy's.

And here they were again.

Adam turned his head away as William's lips descended, so they hit his cheek instead of their intended target.

"Are you still playing hard to get?" There was an edge to William's voice. Adam wondered if it was new or if it had always been there and he simply hadn't noticed it before.

"Not playing anything." Adam was tempted to push through the gate of Harry's backyard, but he knew William would follow. That deflected kiss wouldn't be allowed to stand.

He shouldn't have accepted William's invitation to brunch. Not after last night. The concert had been, for a moment, so wonderful. Well, not the concert. Freddy.

He'd agreed to brunch because he'd decided he needed to break things off with William—not that there were really "things" to break off. There had only been a handful of kisses. A few restaurant meals. Some not-unpleasant time spent together.

But he couldn't do it anymore.

When Freddy had been about to suggest—Adam thought— that they go out for fish and chips, Adam's heart had...woken up. It was the only way he could think to describe it. Like it was coming out of hibernation. He'd been so excited. Flooded with giddy anticipation and nerves and yearning.

That's what a date should feel like.

Not like this. This...lack of unpleasantness.

And when William had swooped in just as Freddy was talking and touched Adam? Well, Adam had been mortified. *I'm not his!* He'd wanted to stand on a chair and yell that at everyone—but mostly at Freddy. But of course that wasn't done. So he'd sat there. Frozen. *Again.*

He hadn't quite been able to work up the nerve to break things off with William at brunch, though, despite the fact that that had been the whole point of the thing. Suddenly, the restaurant hadn't seemed the place. He didn't want to embarrass William—or himself—in a public setting.

But what the hell? Had he always been this much of a coward? Who cared what people thought? He didn't owe these people anything—certainly not "good behavior."

All good behavior had done all these years was make him miserable.

Anger surged through him. He'd always blamed himself, rather than Rusty, for what happened with Freddy. He still did. But all of a sudden all his regret hardened into rage. All the sad, passive wistfulness he'd been carrying around all these years slid away like a skin being shed to reveal a stronger, suppler interior that must have been there all along.

That must have been what Freddy had seen.

I don't belong here.

It was time to go home. Start living his life. Even if it wasn't the life he wanted, it was *his.* It was time he started acting like it.

He turned to William. "Actually, maybe I have been playing hard to get. But only because I *am* hard to get. I'm not really…available."

"There's someone else?"

"Yes. No. Well, not in the way you mean." He shook his head. "It doesn't matter. The point is, I can't—"

"Save it."

In another context, the reaction might have been masking pain, but that wasn't what was happening here. If Adam had gotten hints before, of something inside William that didn't match the way he presented, a flash of impatience or a touch of disingenuousness, that intuition had been correct. Because he was no longer hiding his impatience. Or his disgust. He threw up his hands, turned, outright sneered, and walking backward, said, "Tell your mother and sister to be out of the house by the end of the week."

And then he was gone.

Adam laughed a little. Because that had been so anticlimactic. And because he felt good.

Also, there was confirmation of why his mother was so invested in the idea of him with William: William was her link to free luxury housing. And now he'd severed it.

He laughed again as he unlatched the gate and stepped into the backyard. Because he still felt good.

"Well, that was a stupid thing to do."

Adam turned toward the voice. "Rusty." He had to learn to start scanning the pool deck for eavesdroppers—and by *eavesdroppers*, he meant *Rusty*.

But not really, because he was leaving. Going home to start living his life in the open, the way he wanted to. So there would be no need to worry about eavesdroppers.

Also? He didn't care what Rusty thought anymore. Well, that wasn't true. He loved Rusty, and his opinion was important to Adam. But he was done letting it dictate his life.

"Sorry, Adam." The apology came from Harry, who was seated next to Rusty. "I told him we should slink away."

"It doesn't matter," Adam said.

"How can you say that?" Rusty started to get up. "You had

William Ellison, a hugely talented and rich man about town, interested in you, and you just went and—"

"Hang on, now," Harry said. "William Ellison? The wine guy? *That's* who you've been seeing, Adam? Jesus Christ, I *knew* that voice was familiar."

"Yes, the wine guy." Rusty looked at Adam. "The wine guy who was your ticket out of Bishop's Glen."

"I don't want to get out of Bishop's Glen, Rusty." Adam had said that to his mentor before, dozens of time. But whatever shift he'd felt inside himself earlier must have been reflected in his words, because Rusty's eyes widened as if he'd really *heard* Adam for the first time. "In fact, I'm going home."

He started for the pool house, and Rusty scoffed. "Now?"

An idea dawned. It was probably a bad one, a Hail Mary pass that would go nowhere, but he had to try. "Tomorrow, actually. I have…something I have to do first."

"Adam," Harry said, "you should know—"

"Well, *I'm* not going home." Rusty spoke over Harry, ignoring his attempt to interject.

"That's okay," Adam said, because it was. "I'll go by myself. I have some stuff I need to get done in town before the shop reopens anyway." Namely, find somewhere to park the RV that wasn't Mark's. A place that was his, even if it was in a shitty trailer park with no trees. And Mr. Collins, who was boarding with Mrs. Littleton and had probably had just about enough of his purebred forebears, deserved some nice, long walks.

"William Ellison, Adam. I don't know what you more want. If you think—"

"William Ellison is married." Harry's interruption was successful this time, and he got their attention with that bomb. Then he dropped another one. "To a woman."

"What?" Rusty whirled on his friend. "That's impossible."

"No it isn't. Her name is Ginny. The winery up there is actually her family's. William married in. She runs things up there, and he handles sales and distribution."

"What?" This time Rusty's question was smaller, infused with doubt.

Adam watched the exchange with detached interest. He should probably be surprised. Nothing about William had suggested he was married, much less to a woman. But then, there had been something off about him, so why couldn't it be this?

"This is what he does," Harry said. "He keeps a boyfriend on the side down here. A younger one. I'm not really sure how he gets away with it, because he's not very subtle about it. All I can think is he and his wife must have an arrangement."

"You're fucking kidding me." Horror had replaced doubt in Rusty's tone.

Harry shrugged. "He must get off on the chase as much as anything. One of my servers got entangled with him for a year or so a while back. It was a disaster. The kid ended up totally heartbroken."

Adam laughed. Not at the heartbroken kid, but at…he wasn't even sure. Himself, maybe. He'd been so angry at himself earlier. Now he was just amused. How had he lost sight of himself so much that he'd almost fallen into the trap of married-to-a-woman Hamptons Ken? It was so ridiculous that all he could do was laugh.

"Adam, I'm sorry," Rusty said. "I had no idea."

"It's okay," Adam said.

"Still." Rusty looked shaken. "I called that one wrong, I guess."

"If you want to make it up to me, get my mom and sister

over here. I need to evict them from their house." He laughed again—this new laughing thing was…kind of awesome, actually. "And I have a few things to tell them before I leave tomorrow."

"How about farewell cocktails here tomorrow afternoon?" Harry asked. "They can take a look at the pool house. They're welcome to move in there for a bit."

Adam shot a look at Rusty. "I don't think you and Wilhelmina will make good roommates."

Rusty looked away. He seemed…embarrassed? Could that be right? That wasn't something Adam had ever seen on Rusty.

"I'm, uh, moving into the big house." He was definitely embarrassed. The way he sort of half smiled at Harry but then quickly looked away was a sure tell. "I kind of already have. You probably haven't noticed because you go to bed so early."

Adam's jaw went slack as Harry—whose chair, now that Adam thought about it, was awfully close to Rusty's—took Rusty's hand. *Wow.*

But why was he so surprised? Rusty had alluded to a teenage romance with Harry, had told him they'd reconnected recently. "Well," he said, struggling to find words. "Congratulations?"

Harry grinned and brought Rusty's hand up to his mouth and kissed it.

"How long are you…staying?" Adam asked.

Rusty shrugged, even as Harry said, "As long as I can hold on to him."

"Harry just retired," Rusty said. "And I'm getting up there. So we're just going to see where things go."

"What about the shop?" Adam asked.

"Well, you're going back, aren't you?"

"Yeah, but you didn't know that, and…" Well, crap, there was no point in arguing. He *was* going back. And he was going to need money. There was going to be a nice backlog of work.

"I'll take you off salary," Rusty said. "We can profit share. You get seventy-five percent while you're there alone." He glanced at Harry. "If I come back, we'll go fifty-fifty, and when I retire, you can buy me out. How does that sound?"

Adam blinked. It sounded great, actually. He'd find a spot to move the RV, and he'd work at the shop—the shop that would be part his.

And maybe… No. He wouldn't allow himself to think about that yet. He was going to try, and what would happen would happen. He had to be okay either way.

The only part about this sudden gift being dropped in his lap he couldn't quite wrap his brain around was… "I thought your whole goal in life was to get me to leave Bishop's Glen? And now you're giving me a stake in the shop?"

"I'm not just sorry about William," Rusty said quietly. He glanced at Harry, who nodded encouragingly at him. "I'm sorry I pushed you so hard in general. And when it came to Freddy specifically. I should have let you make your own mistakes. I was just trying…" He blew out a frustrated breath.

Looking at the pair of them, huddled so closely together, Adam thought he finally got it. "Rusty, is it possible that when you were talking all those years about me being trapped in Bishop's Glen, you weren't talking about me at all?"

"It's possible." Rusty's eyes filled with tears. "I just didn't want you to make the same mistakes I did."

"I'm the one who made the mistake." Harry's tone was vehement, but his voice was shaky. "I'm the one who said I was coming back. I'm the one who kept you waiting there."

"The point," Rusty said, shaking his head to forestall more

speech from Harry, "is that we've all learned something." He rolled his eyes, and suddenly Lady Merlot was back. *"Hopefully* we've learned something."

"And what have we learned?" Adam asked. When the question earned him a bigger eye roll, he added, "Humor me."

"We've learned," said Rusty, looking between Adam and Harry with affection in his eyes, "not to let anything or anyone persuade us not to go after what—and who—we want."

Right. That was exactly right. He turned to Harry. "Hey, any chance I can get you to do some detective work for me?"

CHAPTER SEVENTEEN

Freddy didn't realize someone was knocking on the door to his motel room at first because he thought it was coming from inside his head.

Oh, his head. *Why* had he thought it was a good idea to chase last night's phone call with Sophie with even *more* whiskey? Hadn't he learned yet that you couldn't drink away a broken heart?

He rolled over, ignoring whoever was outside. He was paid up through the end of the week, and the only person who knew where he was staying was Bronwen, who, God love her, would never darken the door of the extremely euphemistically named East Hampton Surf "Resort." So whoever it was had the wrong room. Wrong guy.

Groaning, he rolled over. The only cure for him right now was more sleep.

But then of course his phone started buzzing.

It would be his sister, with her bullshit carpe diem homilies about pride and the meaning of life.

Fuck. He felt around for the phone on the nightstand,

turned it off without looking at it, threw it on the floor, stuck his head underneath his pillow, and went back to sleep.

Two hours later, feeling slightly less close to death, he got up, showered, and headed out in search of breakfast.

And tripped over...a takeout container of fish and chips that had been left outside his door?

What the hell?

It was from that place up the coast, the one he'd been telling Adam about. He recognized the newspaper sticking out of the container—an old-school touch he'd appreciated when he ate there in person.

Suddenly shaky—and not from the hangover—he crouched and opened the container. There was a note inside, nestled on top of the now-cold cod.

Sorry I missed you. —Adam.

Heart jackhammering, he rose and took out his phone. There were two unread texts, and they weren't from his sister.

```
Not to sound like a stalker or anything, but
I'm outside your motel room door.
```

Then, a couple minutes later:

```
Okay, I'm heading home to Bishop's Glen
today. Take care, Freddy.
```

Freddy looked around frantically, but that was stupid. Adam had been here hours ago. He'd probably thought Freddy was out or—

No. His gaze snagged on the window to his room—the

window with the curtain half-open. Making his way over to it, he peered in. There was a clear view of the bed.

Adam would have been able to see him there. And, when he didn't answer the door or respond to the text—no, when he saw Freddy pick up his phone and angrily fling it away from the bed—he would have thought he was ignoring him on purpose. That he didn't want to see him.

No. No.

Sophie was right. His pride was holding him back. His pride was standing in the way of what he wanted—needed—to be happy.

His pride could go fuck itself.

Leaping over the fish and chips like a deranged hurdler, Freddy took off running.

"Oh, no, no, no. This won't do at all. It's entirely too small."

Wilhelmina led the way out of the second bedroom in Harry's pool house, the one that had been Adam's but which currently housed only his packed suitcase.

"Entirely too small." Betsy echoed Wilhelmina's assessment.

"It's also free." Adam opened the door and ushered them outside to the pool deck. The quicker to say what he needed to say so he could leave. He honestly didn't care one way or the other whether they took Harry up on his more-than-generous offer to let them stay in the pool house for a few weeks.

His mother glared at him as she marched out the door. Once outside, she turned and folded her arms. "And so was our last place, but *you* screwed things up with William."

"Things didn't work out between us," Adam agreed cheer-fully. "He's kind of a repulsive human being, actually."

"*Adam.* How can you *say* that?"

He shrugged. "Because it's true?" It was amazing, actually, how easy it was to tell the truth once you started. Easy—and liberating.

"You're being completely irrational. If you had just gotten your hair cut or, I don't know, developed some taste in men—"

"You know what, Mother?" Another thing that was turning out to be easy? Interrupting his mother when she was talking nonsense.

She put her hands on her hips. "What?" She didn't even bother trying to temper the disgust in her tone.

"I actually have excellent taste in men. I've only ever loved one of them, and he was a tremendous one. Just because I blew it with him doesn't mean there's anything wrong with my taste. Only my judgment."

Betsy gasped. Wilhelmina started marching toward the gate. "I can't listen to this anymore."

Adam followed. "I have one more thing to say."

She stopped with her hand on the gate, clearly not seeing the need to bother with eye contact. Which was fine. He didn't need that.

"I'm going to go back home now," he said. "And I'm still going to love you and all that. You're my mother. I'll always love you. But all that doesn't make what I'm going to say next any less true. I should have said this years ago." He paused. Not because he was hesitating, but because he was relishing. Having it on the tip of his tongue, not quite out in the world but about to be, was the most delicious thing.

She did turn then, her eyebrows raised.

He, Adam Elliot of Kellynch Estates, let it rip. "Fuck. You."

Holy fuck.

Holy, holy, holy *fuck.*

Freddy barely made it around the corner, out of sight of the gate before Wilhelmina and Betsy Elliot swept through it, floating away on a cloud of indignation.

He slumped against the fence. Then, when the wall behind him still didn't feel solid enough to keep him on his feet, he sank to the ground

I actually have excellent taste in men. I've only ever loved one of them, and he was a tremendous one.

Was Freddy interpreting that correctly?

Closing his eyes to block out any distraction, he went back over the conversation—confrontation, really—he'd just over-heard between Adam and his mother.

Was there any chance he'd been talking about that shit-head William Ellison?

No. Freddy was pretty sure William Ellison wasn't getting fish and chips delivered to his door.

What now? He'd run over here in a panic, afraid Adam would have already left town. But he hadn't. He was here. Just over the fence. Probably with Rusty. What the hell was Freddy supposed to do now? The panic wasn't subsiding. Adam was the one who was good with words.

Okay, he needed to get his shit together. He was here because he'd decided to set aside his pride. To see if letting go of it for a while would allow him to speak what was in his heart. Because God knew, there was pride and there was…life. And he didn't know anymore how to live without Adam.

He didn't want to be in New York City. He didn't want to be in the Hamptons.

He wanted to be under the stars inside Adam's RV.

He picked up his phone.

The first text came as Adam was loading his suitcase into his rental car for the trip home.

```
I need to talk to you.
```

Oh, God. Freddy. He'd assumed Freddy was done with him after he'd blown him off at the motel, but there was the text clearly labeled "Freddy Wentworth" upending him with six innocuous little words.

He was trying to get his clumsy fingers to bang out a reply, something along the lines of *Anytime* when more texts started coming. One after the other, a long stream of them, like Freddy was hitting send after every thought.

```
I don't know if this feeling inside me is
hope or despair. It's all mixed up.
```

```
I hope this isn't too late.
```

```
I'm just going to say this, as hard as it
is: I want you back.
```

```
I told everyone I came to the Hamptons
because I was thinking of opening a restau-
rant here, but it was a lie. I came here
```

because you were here.

I can hardly type.

I've never loved anyone but you.

I've been so angry at you. So hurt. But I've always loved you.

I still love you.

Freddy dropped his phone after the last text. He couldn't see anymore through the tears that had gathered in his eyes.

But then the sound of a wail from the other side of the fence electrified him—he'd forgotten one important logistical detail in that epic string of texts, something along the lines of *By the way, I'm right outside.*

He was having trouble making it to his feet—his legs felt made of cement—when his phone buzzed.

I love you, too. There's never been anyone else for me. I'm sorry. I'm so sorry I threw away so many years.

The gate crashed open, and Adam ran—as well as he could —out of it, went loping down the sidewalk.

The sight of Adam receding into the distance galvanized Freddy. He was off running in a heartbeat, caught up with Adam in two.

"Hey," he said as Adam slowed to a halt and turned to him with wide eyes.

Then his mouth went dry, and they stood there staring at each other, Adam panting from running, Freddy panting from…hope? Happiness? Whatever it was, it was unfamiliar, and it had taken up residence in the center of his chest, rapidly expanding as it crowded out his lungs.

Adam's eyes went even wider, and they were getting shiny.

Shit. He had to say something here. So he said the first thing that popped into his mind. "Wherever you're going, can I walk you?"

It was the right thing, because although a tear slipped out of the corner of one of Adam's eyes, he smiled. "I was actually going to go home. I have a rental car, and it's all packed."

Home. Freddy nodded. That sounded right, too. "Yeah. Let's go home."

He opened his arms, and Adam stepped into them.

EPILOGUE

Six months later

"Get up, sleepyhead. It's a big day."

Adam twisted away to silence the alarm clock and then came back and burrowed into Freddy's chest. His favorite place in the world.

"I'm still not used to this," Freddy murmured sleepily.

"Used to what?" Adam pressed kisses against Freddy's jaw to wake him up. They had a lot to do today. He had to be at the shop in an hour, and Freddy had a meeting with the contractor to sign off on the final touches on the little log cabin they were building adjacent to the woods at Kellynch. Then he would have to scramble to open the food truck in time for lunch.

Freddy grinned and pulled Adam on top of him. "To being happier than I deserve. To sleeping with you every night under these stars." He nodded up at the ceiling.

"You deserve to be happy," said Adam, and before he could say anything else, Freddy had stopped his mouth with a kiss.

Freddy always knew when he was about to try to apologize again for all the years they'd spent apart. He let his tongue slide leisurely into Adam's mouth, and they sighed against each other for a few moments.

Then Freddy pulled away and said what he always said when he was reading Adam's mind: "Those years got us here."

Yes, they had. And *here* was a lovely place to be.

Freddy had gotten into Adam's car that day in the Hamptons and driven home with him. Stayed with him, minus a few trips to New York to ease himself out, legally and logistically, of Captain's Manhattan and into Captain's Grilled Cheese, which was currently parked at the Kellynch lakeshore, serving Sophie and Geordie's boating customers before and after their cruises. There had been a lot of demand for the truck at other wineries and at local festivals, but they were taking things slow.

Adam had tried to insist that they buy a proper house, but Freddy wasn't having it. In the end, they'd come up with an ingenious solution. And tonight was the night they would implement it. Adam grinned when he thought about it.

"What?" Freddy teased, kissing him on the nose.

"What what?"

"Why are *you* so happy?"

Adam rolled his eyes. "Do you need me to count the ways?"

"Well, if I recall, you have to work on Mrs. Littleton's car this morning. That can't be happy-making."

"Eh, I'm going to have Karen do it."

Karen had come to the shop via the high school career fair last spring. It turned out that although Adam had bailed on it in favor of dinner at Ben's, Rusty had managed to staff both the automotive and drag booths. Karen was smart and enthusiastic, and Adam's not-so-secret plan was to gradually give her more and more responsibility. As full owner of Anderson Motors, he had that power. Rusty had remained in the Hamptons, and by all accounts, he and Harry, making up for lost time, were more in love than ever. Adam had bought Rusty out and was now solely in charge at the auto shop.

Adam liked the auto shop. He always had, and he still did. So he would probably always keep some hand in the goings-on there, but the long-term plan was for him to become less involved and for Karen to gradually take over the day-to-day operations. Maybe someday he'd cut her a stake, as Rusty had done with him.

The idea behind him being less involved at Anderson was to free him up for other pursuits: namely, winemaking.

For now, Captain's Grilled Cheese was serving wine from other local vineyards, but Sophie, Geordie, Freddy, and Adam had put their heads together and decided on a plan to get Kellynch up and running again as a functioning winery. They'd cut Freddy in as a partner—his contribution was running the food truck and supervising the winemaker they'd hired. They'd found someone with a great track record, and the guy had committed to Kellynch for five years, and this time, there was enough capital to work with. He was going to mentor Adam, who would take on an informal apprentice role. He would bring the viticultural expertise, and Adam would bring the local history and knowledge. They'd all agreed to reassess in five years. If Adam was ready, he would take over as winemaker. If he wasn't, that was okay, too. Mostly, he was just thrilled to know that the family vines would be producing again.

And the best part was that Sophie had insisted that if Freddy and Adam were going to live in Adam's RV—which

Freddy had insisted on—they were going to do it on the grounds at Kellynch.

So Adam was back home.

Freddy stretched, which had the effect of rubbing his morning wood against Adam's thigh.

He was home in more ways than one. He burrowed under the covers.

"Hey, now!" Freddy laughingly protested. "You were the one insisting we had to get up. Big day and all that."

Adam just grunted. He couldn't talk because his mouth was full.

It *was* a big day. And it went agonizingly slowly. He had intended to close the shop early, but a last-minute customer with a flat kept him there later than planned, so it was nearly five by the time he turned up the drive to Kellynch. Because today was a momentous day—and because he'd been running sufficiently late this morning thanks to his morning romp with Freddy—he'd driven to work instead of walking.

Freddy was waiting for him outside. Adam had kind of expected there to be workmen on site, but really there was no reason for that. The house was ready, as was the slab the RV would live on permanently.

Freddy jogged over to help Adam out of the car, which was unnecessary but also so very in character for Freddy. He grinned. "You ready?"

"I am. You?"

"I've got the door off, so we're all ready to go with this bonkers plan."

Adam made to swat him. "Do I need to remind you that this bonkers plan was your idea?" Adam had been more than ready to give up the RV. It really was too small for two people to live in. But Freddy wouldn't hear of it. Hence the bonkers plan.

Freddy captured Adam's hand mid-swat and used it to lever Adam flush with his chest. Adam's pulse raced, as it still did when Freddy was near, even after all these months. He lowered his mouth over Adam's, and Adam's knees wobbled. Freddy, who somehow always knew what Adam needed, banded a strong hand around him to keep him upright. Adam allowed himself to get lost in the kiss for a long moment, but eventually and with great effort, he pulled back. "We have to get moving if we want to do the hookup before it gets dark."

"I'll show you a hookup." Freddy waggled his eyebrows. "But I guess *that* one can wait until *after* dark." He patted Adam's butt before stepping away. "You drive, and I'll direct."

Adam's stomach fluttered with excitement. They'd been talking about this plan for so long and working on the all the incremental steps—ripping the kitchen and some of the built-in furniture out of the RV, getting the slab poured. Not to mention building the house itself.

He felt a pang of missing Rusty as he climbed into the cab of the RV. Lady Merlot would probably say something like, "Come on, pretty boy!" But knowing Rusty was happily ensconced in the Hamptons, he whispered the incantation in Rusty's place and turned the key. The engine roared to life, and happy goosebumps rose on his skin.

He stuck his head out the window. "I'm going to back up a ways so I can drive straight up onto the slab."

Mr. Collins, who'd been napping under a tree, started yapping up a storm at the sight of the RV in motion.

Freddy walked backward and positioned himself so he could see the point at which the RV's doorway would line up with a hallway that extended from the new log cabin. It functioned kind of like a Jetway linking a plane to an airport terminal. The idea was to line up the hole on the RV where the door used to be with the hallway. Then they'd lower the RV onto jacks and take off the tires, and they had a contractor coming tomorrow to seal the opening where RV met hallway. They'd turned the RV into a deluxe master suite/library— Freddy said he wanted to sleep under the fake stars every night for the rest of his life. The other side—the cabin— contained a large designer kitchen and a large designer bathroom with a giant-ass soaker tub—both by Freddy's request. The main living space, they'd made small and cozy—like Ben's log cabin but on a more intimate scale. Exposed logs, a fireplace, comfy furniture. Outside, Freddy had already roughed in a garden he would plant later this spring—he was going to try to grow some of the produce he would use in the food truck.

There would also be peonies. Lots and lots of peonies.

It was almost too perfect to bear. Almost. Adam had a feeling he would find a way to manage.

"Whoa!" Freddy held up a hand. "You've overshot a little. Back up maybe six inches."

A little more to-ing and fro-ing, and the RV was in place. Adam leaned out the window. "I think I left my toolbox in the house when I was helping your sister hang some pictures last week. You want to run get it, and we can get these tires off?"

Freddy waved off the suggestion. Stared silently at Adam for a long time. When he finally spoke, his voice was gruff. "Let's do the tires tomorrow. You go through the RV, and I'll go through the house, and we'll meet in the middle."

Adam was too choked up to speak, suddenly, so he nodded. He made his way through the RV, marveling anew at how amazing the place looked. The bed was still in the nook, but without the kitchen, the space was open and airy. There was a little seating area with a small TV, and more bookshelves. He'd left the plants, at Freddy's insistence, though they'd started making cuttings so they could adorn the cabin with greenery, too. Many of the surfaces were littered with the beginnings of new plants in water. He looked forward to bringing them across.

Adam's new life had somehow retained all best parts of his old life—the RV, Kellynch—plus…Freddy.

"What's the hold up?" Freddy shouted. And if Adam had been distracted by the lump in his throat, he was cured of that when Freddy added, "Get your fine ass over here!"

It was a little out of character for Freddy to summon him by yelling. Usually if he wanted Adam to go somewhere, he was the perfect mixture of chivalry and filth, slipping his hand into Adam's but then leavening that gentlemanliness by whispering something deliciously lewd in his ears. He claimed to love making Adam blush and said that since the first phase of their relationship had been conducted exclusively at night, he'd made it his mission to trigger as many daytime blushes as possible.

He was really good at it.

To wit: Adam was already blushing, for no reason at all, really, when he reached the door of the RV.

They had achieved a pretty snug fit between the RV and the log hallway. The contractor would have a straightforward time of it tomorrow. All that was left was to replace the steps down from the RV with a more permanent set, and they would be—

"Stop admiring our handiwork and come here."

It was hard to stop admiring their handiwork, though, theirs and that of the builders. As Adam walked along the hallway, he ran his hands along the warm red-brown logs that made up the walls. He'd been inside it before, of course, but never like this, never when it was an internal space, connected up to the RV.

It was really something to behold. It was—

"Careful!"

Freddy's hands shot up to steady Adam. *Up* because Freddy himself was on the ground—Adam, who had been busy fondling the walls, had almost tripped over him.

Freddy kept both hands on Adam's waist for a moment and then, seemingly satisfied that Adam had found his equilibrium, he let go with one hand, dug into his front pocket, and produced...

"Your ring?" It was the old wooden ring, the one Freddy had given him that magical night eight years ago. Seeing it took his breath away.

"*Your* ring."

"But—"

"Sophie found it when they had a tree removed from near the barrel room. I should have given it back to you months ago, but—"

"It's not mine."

"It is, though. I made it for you."

"But that's not logical." Freddy used to say that back in the day, too, insist that he'd made the ring for Adam. It had been the sweetest thing then. It was now, too. Adam wasn't sure why he was arguing. "You didn't even know me when you made it."

"I hoped for you." Freddy shrugged. "Same thing."

"You are adorable. I know you don't want to hear that because you're such a badass, but you're adorable. Illogical, too, but—"

"Will you shut up and let me propose?"

Wait. What?

His face must have telegraphed his confusion, because Freddy rolled his eyes good-naturedly and said, "When someone kneels in front of you and hands you a ring—in your brand-new house that you're going to live in together—what do you think is happening?"

He might as well have turned on a tap, because tears just started leaking out the side of Adam's eyes.

"Oh, shit!" Freddy jumped to his feet. "Don't cry."

Adam waved him off, wiped his eyes, and ordered himself to get his act together. "It's happy crying."

"So that means you're going to say yes?"

Adam chuckled even as a few stray tears fell. "I don't know. What was the question again?"

"The question was 'Will you marry me?' There was a speech before that, too. Do you want to hear it?"

"You'd better believe it."

"Well, I was going to say that the first night I walked you back to Kellynch was the best night of my life. But I actually think maybe it was the day my sister texted me that she'd found this ring." He held it up between them. "Because it came with a sisterly lecture about not letting pride get in the way of what I truly wanted."

"And what did you truly want?"

"You. You're all I've ever wanted. And then I woke up and found those fish and chips, and it was like—"

"I'm so sorry—"

He held up a hand. "No more apologies. I wasn't blameless. You were too easily swayed by Rusty and your family, but I was too proud. I ran off and changed my phone number and never looked back. Was incapable of entertaining the idea that you could change your mind. But I learned. You did, too. I heard you tell off your mother that day. We *both* learned our lessons. Would we have learned them if we'd stayed together?"

It was a good question. "Maybe we had to lose each other first. Maybe we had to feel how high the stakes were."

"Like leaving and coming home again on your own terms."

That was it. That was exactly what they were doing. That's why Adam had been so fixated on the walls earlier. He had a home back at Kellynch again. A bigger, transformed version of everything he'd loved about his home before. He suspected Freddy felt the same. The chip on his shoulder was mostly gone—he was still a little grumbly about Bishop's Glen, but Freddy's grumbly-ness was part of his charm. And he was doing the kind of cooking and food growing that felt right to him right now.

But it wasn't just true about the house. Adam had lost Freddy, too, and then found him again. And like the house, his heart was bigger and stronger for it, even if it was cobbled together from some previously broken bits.

And here was one more thing he'd lost that had miraculously come back to him—the ring.

Freddy held it out. "I love you so much. I never want to be anywhere else but here in this shithole of a town, with you. What do you say?"

"I say yes. Of course. Yes."

Freddy's hands shook as he closed the ring into Adam's palm. "I can make you a new one that actually fits."

"I want this one," Adam said, his voice reflecting the fierceness with which the sentiment arose in his heart. "I'll wear it around my neck like before, except outside my clothes this time."

But maybe Freddy wanted to see Adam wearing a proper ring on his finger—he did have that throwback chivalry thing going. Adam could be down with that—very down with that. "Is it weird to just wear it around my neck? I could maybe do both—keep this as a necklace and get a proper ring?"

"Nah. Not weird. We can do what we want."

"We can do what we want," Adam echoed. It was such a lovely sentiment. Hard-earned, too, and all the more treasured for it.

"However," Freddy said, "there's one thing we have to do —go to the store for brunch fixings and champagne, because I invited your family over for a celebratory brunch tomorrow."

"You *did*?" While Freddy got along okay with Mark and Betsy—Freddy's wealth and fame had conferred a kind of amnesia on Adam's siblings—Wilhelmina had not budged. She was as frosty as ever toward Freddy, probably because she couldn't admit that she'd been wrong all those years ago.

Which was fine. Adam didn't have the same kind of relationship with his family anymore. He still loved them—he always would—but he'd freed himself from their orbit. And once he'd stopped feeling responsible for them—and for pleasing them—they'd receded in importance.

Also there was the part where they were busy—they'd finally had to get jobs. Ha. Adam couldn't help but take a twisted kind of delight in that aspect of things. When William turned on them, they'd come back to Bishop's Glen and rented a place in town. Adam had financed a stint in cosmetology school for Betsy, and she'd gotten a job at a local spa, where she was known for her elaborate nail designs. Wilhelmina had been working at a boutique, and after doing up the store's holiday window, she'd stumbled into some interior design gigs and was gradually building up her own business. Which was pretty much perfect for her—her penchant for appearances and for having things just so was finally being monetized. Adam suspected they probably still lived way above their means, but he was making that not his problem anymore.

Because of his mother's treatment of Freddy, they didn't see her very often. Freddy tried, knowing it was important to Adam, but honestly, Adam wasn't okay with it. So he sometimes met his mother for lunch in town, but for the most part, he kept her where she belonged—in a secondary role. Freddy had told him all those years ago to choose, and he'd finally made the right choice.

So it was a bit surprising that Freddy had invited her for brunch. "You just called her up and invited her over?"

"Yep. I believe my exact words were 'Come over to the low-classy house on wheels in which I'm debauching your son on a nightly basis for a celebration.'"

"How did you know I'd say yes?" Adam teased.

Freddy smirked. "I didn't tell her what the celebration was for. She probably thinks it's just about the new house." He laughed snarkily. "She is going to lose her mind when she finds out we're engaged."

"We're engaged!" Adam exclaimed.

"We're engaged," Freddy echoed, looking very pleased with himself. But then his face grew serious. "And really, though I will enjoy the hell out of telling her that, I just thought you might like to celebrate everything with your family. I invited Sophie and Geordie, too."

"It sounds perfect. Thank you."

"So what do you think? Grilled cheese and champagne?"

"Perfect. Let's go." Adam fished out his keys. "You want me to drive?"

"Nah. Let's walk."

At the sound of the w-word, Mr. Collins started jumping so furiously, he was practically levitating. Freddy rolled his eyes but clipped a leash on the beast.

Then he grabbed Adam's hand, and they walked.

ACKNOWLEDGMENTS

The wonderful phrase "the armpit of the Finger Lakes" comes from my friend Jason Haremza. I'm thankful to Sandra Owens and Julia Ganis for reading early drafts, and to Courtney Miller-Callihan for the fine and steadfast career shepherding. Thanks to the folks at Riptide Publishing for giving this book its start—and for reverting it to me when I asked.

CONNECT WITH ME

Connect with me

Sign up for my newsletter at jennyholiday.com/newsletter. I send newsletters when I have a new release or a sale, and I sometimes include giveaways and access to freebies only for subscribers. Or you can find me on Twitter at @jennyholi or Instagram at @holymolyjennyholi. (I'm technically on Facebook, but I'm rarely actually there.) Visit my website at jennyholiday.com.

Reviews really help authors, not only because they help us find new readers but because more reviews means more favorable treatment by retailers' algorithms. If you're moved to leave an honest review of this book or any of my others on the retailer's site where you bought it, I'd be most grateful.

ABOUT THE AUTHOR

Jenny Holiday started writing at age nine when her awesome fourth grade teacher gave her a notebook and told her to start writing some stories. That first batch featured mass murderers on the loose, alien invasions, and hauntings. (Looking back, she's amazed no one sent her to a kid-shrink.) She's been writing ever since. After a detour to get a PhD in geography, she worked as a professional writer for many years. Later, her tastes having evolved from alien invasions to happily-ever-afters, she tried her hand at romance. Today she is a USA Today bestselling author of all sorts of romance novels: contemporary and historical, straight and gay. She lives in London, Ontario.

www.jennyholiday.com
jenny@jennyholiday.com
Twitter: @jennyholi
Instagram: @holymolyjennyholi
Newsletter: jennyholiday.com/newsletter

OTHER BOOKS BY JENNY HOLIDAY

THE FAMOUS SERIES

Famous

Infamous (a male/male romance)

BRIDESMAIDS BEHAVING BADLY

One and Only

It Takes Two

Merrily Ever After

Three Little Words

THE 49TH FLOOR

Saving the CEO

Sleeping With Her Enemy

The Engagement Game

His Heart's Revenge (a male/male romance)

NEW WAVE NEWSROOM

The Fixer

The Gossip

The Pacifist

REGENCY REFORMERS

The Miss Mirren Mission

The Likelihood of Lucy

Viscountess of Vice

AN EXCERPT FROM INFAMOUS

Available everywhere ebooks are sold, and in paperback from Amazon. Read on for an excerpt.

Is he brave enough to face the music?

All that up-and-coming musician Jesse Jamison has ever wanted is to be on the cover of *Rolling Stone*. When a gossip website nearly catches him kissing someone who isn't his famous girlfriend—and also isn't a girl—he considers the near miss a wake-up call. There's a lot riding on his image as the super-straight rocker, and if he wants to realize his dreams, he'll need to toe the line. Luckily, he's into women too. Problem solved.

After a decade pretending to be his ex's roommate, pediatrician Hunter Wyatt is done hiding. He might not know how to date in the Grindr world, how to make friends in a strange city, or whether his new job in Toronto is a mistake. But he does know that no one is worth the closet. Not even the world's sexiest rock star.

As Jesse's charity work at Hunter's hospital brings the two closer together, a bromance develops. Soon, Hunter is all Jesse can think about. But when it comes down to a choice between Hunter and his career, he's not sure he's brave enough to follow his heart.

CHAPTER ONE

At the last second, Jesse changed his mind and sat next to the hot guy instead of the middle-aged businesswoman.

It was a breach of the rules. Jesse had been taking the Sunday afternoon Montreal-to-Toronto train once a month for the past four years, and he had a system, a well-honed methodology developed from painful trial and error.

And by *painful*, he meant, for example, *five hours trapped next to a young mother holding a teething baby.*

Most people liked to rush onto the train as soon as possible, and they aggressively went after empty rows, seating themselves alone. But this route always sold out. Since the train was going to fill, it was smarter to hang back a bit, to bide his time and get onto a car that looked like it was about half-full. That way, he could choose his seatmate, whereas all those hasty people alone in two-seater rows had to resign themselves to a journey with whoever happened to plop down next to them.

No, it was infinitely preferable to be in control of one's own destiny.

And Jesse was nothing if not in control of his destiny.

So whenever Jesse got on a train, the first thing he always did was start profiling the hell out of potential seatmates.

Middle-aged women were the best. Even better if they looked like they were traveling on business. If they *also* wore wedding rings? Jackpot. Women in general tended not to initiate conversation and left him to pass the time in peace, the aforementioned mother-of-teether being emblematic of an exceptional subcategory: mothers desperately in need of adult conversation.

Another subcategory to avoid regardless of gender? The elderly, God bless them, were not ideal seatmates.

Neither were teenagers, the ultimate undesirables. They were starting to recognize him. Some people in their twenties and thirties did too, but they usually couldn't remember from where—or if they did, it sparked a brief conversation and then they picked up on his not-so-subtle cues and left him alone. But if a teenaged girl recognized him, he was doomed. He generally didn't like to think of teenagers as the band's target demographic, but you never had any idea what the record label was going to do with your stuff. Before you knew it, you'd be appearing on Spotify playlists called "teen heartbreak" or some shit.

He was beginning to think it was time to arrange alternate transportation for his monthly trips back from Montreal. Things were happening faster on the career front than he'd anticipated. By the time he was on the cover of *Rolling Stone*, he wasn't going to be taking the train anymore anyway. And what do they say? "Start as you mean to go on"?

Today, he ambled down the aisle, scanning the rows until he spied the perfect target: midforties, hair blown out into a perfect dark-brown helmet, business suit, laptop already fired up.

As he approached, he surveyed the rest of the car. The row across from the businesswoman was occupied by a man reading a book. He was dressed in an aqua button-down shirt and dark jeans. Salt-and-pepper hair, which was clearly premature—the guy couldn't have been more than thirty-five—swooshed back into a messy pompadour that was shorter on the sides. His most prominent facial feature was a chiseled jaw dusted with a few days' worth of beard growth that was more salt than pepper.

Well, shit. A baby silver fox.

The poor bastard would probably end up with some clingy woman sitting next to him, projecting all her hopes onto him for the duration of the trip.

Jesse should do a good deed and sit next to him.

He usually tried to ignore men who weren't obviously working on something. You never knew with men. It was harder to make snap judgments about them. Sometimes they kept to themselves, but sometimes the newspaper they'd seemed so engrossed in would turn out to be a prop and they'd want to buddy up with you.

Someone was coming up the aisle behind him. Jesse was holding everyone up.

The woman was safer. Infinitely safer.

He set his bag down on the seat next to the man.

Jesse rummaged through it to pull out the items he'd need during the trip—phone, bottle of water, the latest issues of *Billboard* and *Rolling Stone*. It was hard not to sigh over the talentless, manufactured boy band on the cover of the latter. But he would have his turn someday.

As he reached up to stash his bag on the overhead shelf, the man looked up and caught his eye.

Jesse nodded as he sat. The man's eyes were striking—a

kind of light brown flecked with gold, bright enough to be visible behind his black horn-rimmed glasses. The silver hair and the almost-gold eyes were a weird but compelling combination, like clashing jewelry.

The man gave a slight smile and said, "Hey," before returning his attention to his book. A second later, though, his phone dinged. He picked it up and eyed the screen. Jesse watched him key in his passcode and read a long text. His eyes seemed to darken in real time, becoming a little less gold, like the sun dimming. He dropped the phone carelessly into the seat pocket in front of him, closed his eyes, and mouthed, *Fuck*.

Some part of Jesse's brain could sense some other part of his brain gearing up to speak.

Don't do it.

They had a five-hour journey ahead of them.

Don't do it.

"Everything okay?"

Damn it.

The man's eyes flew open as the rational part Jesse's brain railed at the mouth-controlling part, which had apparently gone rogue.

"Sorry," Jesse said, and what was he *doing*? This way lay ruin. Or at least the possibility of an excruciatingly tedious five hours, because who knew if he'd been brainwashed by this guy's good looks? "You just seemed...upset all of a sudden."

The man opened his mouth, then closed it, like maybe he was at war with himself too.

"Sorry," said Jesse again, which was weird because *Spin*'s review of the band's last record had called it "unapologetic," and never had Jesse been more satisfied with an adjective. "I'll leave you alone."

You know the best way to leave someone alone? Leave them the fuck alone.

"I'm a doctor," the man said, kind of woodenly, like he was trying out this talking thing for the first time. His voice was all gravel and velvet, which should have been a contradiction, but apparently a guy with silver hair and gold eyes didn't have to hew to the rules that governed the rest of the slobs in the world. "A pediatrician. I have a patient who got some bad news."

"Yeah?" Jesse prompted, because suddenly, he could no longer imagine anything he'd like to do more for the next five hours than listen to Baby Silver Fox talk about his job. Also: what the hell?

"He needs a new liver. We were testing his brother as a possible donor." He looked out the window at the passing scenery as he spoke. "It was this kid's best hope. That was one of the nurses texting with the news that the brother is not a match. Now he's got to sit around on the waiting list biding time—and time isn't something this kid has a ton of." He ran his hands through his hair, scraping his fingers against his scalp in frustration as he turned his attention back to Jesse. "Sorry. That was probably a longer answer than you wanted."

Christ. That put things into perspective, didn't it? Here Jesse was, his biggest problem that he wasn't making enough money to fly back from Montreal after his visits with his sister but he was starting to be recognized on the train. "You know what? I'll be right back." He popped up and hunted down the porter, who hadn't begun food and beverage service yet and, by dangling an enormous tip, managed to procure two tiny bottles of whiskey.

When he plunked them down on Baby Silver Fox's tray, it

occurred to him that maybe whiskey wasn't the best answer to *liver problems*, but the man grinned and said, "It's noon somewhere?"

"Exactly," said Jesse, a fierce sort of satisfaction lodging in his chest at the idea that he'd made this man smile. "Nothing like a little midmorning whiskey to take your mind off your problems." He twisted open one of the bottles and handed it over, belatedly wishing he'd gotten something classier than whiskey. This guy probably drank martinis.

"Thanks." Baby Silver Fox clinked his bottle against Jesse's and then took a sip.

He wasn't sure what to say. "So you're a pediatrician? That must be rewarding." As soon as it was out, though, he regretted it. *The guy tells you a kid is on the verge of death, and you say, "How rewarding"?* "On the whole, I mean. Making kids well," he added, because why stop while he was behind?

"I wish. Most of the kids I see are really sick. I work at Toronto Children's Hospital. I'm a hospitalist. You know what that is? Most people don't."

"I would be one of those people."

"It's sort of like a general practitioner, but for patients in the hospital. I oversee their care—many of them are being seen by lots of different kinds of specialists and technicians. I make sure everything is integrated optimally and..." He trailed off and sighed.

"And that kids who need new livers get them?" Jesse finished softly.

Baby Silver Fox—make that *Dr.* Baby Silver Fox—rolled his eyes like he was disgusted with himself. "In theory."

"Hey, now. It's not your fault this kid's brother wasn't a match."

"I know. I'm just... I don't know. I moved to Toronto from

Montreal three months ago. I thought about changing things up when I decided I was going to move—joining a regular pediatric practice. Giving out vaccines and fixing tummy trouble and referring on the hard cases. You'd think stuff like this would get easier, but it doesn't."

"I don't imagine dying kids ever gets easy."

The doctor made a vague noise of agreement. "Sometimes I wonder what I was thinking. The point of moving was to make a fresh start. And here I am doing the exact same thing I was doing in Montreal…and, Jesus, listen to me. I don't even know you, and it's like I think you're my therapist or something." He held up his now-empty bottle. "I'm a bit of a lightweight, I'm afraid. And also a chatty drunk, so…"

"Hey, it's okay." And, amazingly, it was. This was exactly the kind of conversation he normally bent over backward to avoid, but somehow, this time, with this guy, he wanted to know more.

"Let's change the subject," said the man. "What about you? What brought you to Montreal? Or is Montreal home?"

"Nope, headed home to Toronto. I'm in a band. We have a monthly gig in Montreal."

"A band that travels by VIA Rail?" He smiled. "You guys should make a commercial."

"No, the gig's on Friday, and the rest of the band heads back afterward in a couple of vans. My sister and her son live in Montreal, though, so I usually spend the weekend with them and make my own way home on Sunday."

"Would I know your work?"

"I doubt it."

"Try me."

"The band's called Jesse and the Joyride."

"Alas, I don't think I know it. Are you Jesse?"

"Yep. Jesse Jamison." He stuck out his hand.

"Hunter Wyatt."

Hunter Wyatt's hand was soft. Or maybe it was only Jesse's guitar-induced calluses that made it seem so.

Jesse held on a heartbeat too long, lulled for a moment by the rocking of the train and the warm flesh against his own.

Hunter quirked a smile as he pulled away. "It's not every day you meet a rock star on the train. Especially a rock star taking the train because he's so dedicated to his sister. You're a regular saint."

"I'm not a saint. Or a rock star, for that matter." *Yet.* "But, yeah, it's just me and my sister and my nephew—he's three. Our parents are gone. My sister's had a rough couple of years. She's mostly on her own with my nephew."

"Husband left?"

If only he *would* leave, once and for all. "Something like that."

"That's tough. We've all been there." He huffed a bitter laugh. "Some of us more recently than others."

"Ah," Jesse said. "The fresh start. The move to Toronto."

"Officially I came for the job, but...yeah."

"How long had you been together?"

"Eight years."

Jesse whistled. "Wow. I don't think I've ever even made it eight *months* in a relationship." Not even close to eight months, truth be told, but he didn't want to admit that in front of this guy who so clearly had his shit together.

"Not so impressive, really," Hunter said, "given that I have literally nothing to show for it."

"So you were back for a visit this weekend?"

"Yeah, the dog died. My ex called and said this was it, so I came up to...say goodbye, I guess."

"Man, harsh."

"Yeah, the worst part is that the dog died before I got there."

"Your girlfriend leaves you and your dog dies? It's like a country song—a bad country song."

The doctor didn't laugh, just screwed up his face like he was trying to decide something. Then he said, "It's, uh, not a girl."

"The dog is not a girl?"

"The girlfriend is not a girlfriend. He's a boyfriend. *Ex-*boyfriend."

"Right."

Right.

Jesse had been afraid of that.

* * *

This was the part where the rock star would freak out.

Which was fine, because Hunter's dog was dead, his sickest patient was going to keep getting sicker, and his ex, Julian, was still a closet-case bent on sucking all the life out of Hunter.

So a little straight-boy panic induced by accidental proximity to a homo was nothing.

He wasn't into pretending to be anything he wasn't—not anymore, anyway—so the testosterone-oozing musician in the next seat could just feel free to panic.

And he *was* panicking.

But apparently not over the fact that Hunter liked dick.

"Holy shit."

His phone had chimed, and he'd picked it up and was

scrolling through what looked like an article illustrated with pictures. Whatever it was, it wasn't good news.

'Twas the season, apparently.

"Holy *shit*," Jesse said again, closing his eyes and letting his chin fall to his chest.

"What's the matter?" Hunter asked, because it seemed rude to check out now.

Jesse opened his eyes and blew out a long, slow breath. "Well, it's nowhere near as bad as your news. That's a good perspective to remember."

"Less-bad bad news. That sounds delightful right about now. Hit me."

He didn't answer, but he handed over his phone.

It was an article on a website called *GossipTO*, headlined *Jesse Jamison making out with mysterious blond—and she isn't Kylie Cameron.*

He read on. Apparently his seatmate was notorious for his stereotypical rock star ways. Before his current girlfriend—this Kylie person—Jesse had enjoyed the groupie lifestyle, if this site was to be believed. Everyone had been shocked when he'd gotten together with Kylie, the story reported. There was also something in there about a trashed hotel room incident.

"I thought you said you weren't a rock star," Hunter said.

"I'm not. Not really."

Hunter chuckled and read part of the article out loud. "'We all know Jesse likes his sex, drugs, and rock and roll, but'—"

Jesse cut him off. "I mean, I have a band. We're doing pretty well in Canada. No one knows our name in the States. Yet. This"—he gestured toward the phone—"is a sensational-istic, B-list Canadian gossip website. But damn, they're out to get me. I can't do anything without them all over my ass. So I enjoy having a little fun from time to time. It's not like I'm breaking any laws." He quirked a grin. "Mostly."

"So they got you making out with this woman who isn't your girlfriend?"

"Yep."

"And your girlfriend is also some kind of celebrity?"

"She's a model."

Hunter couldn't really see anything about the person Jesse was kissing in the blurry shot. Jesse had his back to the camera, and his companion was leaning against a brick wall. She was as tall as Jesse, and models were tall, right? All that was visible of the kiss-ee was shoulder-length, dirty-blond, almost-messy hair—which also seemed kind of model-esque, in that way that models sometimes seemed to strive to look bad in the name of fashion. "So there's no way this could be her?"

"You don't know Kylie Cameron?" Jesse asked.

Hunter searched his mind. "I don't think so?"

"She's Asian. She has long black hair."

"Ah," Hunter said. "I guess you're busted."

"Yeah, and in addition to that not being her, Kylie is like, Canada's sweetheart. She was on *Degrassi* as a kid—before she moved into modeling."

"I'm kind of out of the pop culture loop," said Hunter, though of course he did know the iconic TV show. Everyone who grew up in Canada knew *Degrassi*. Hell, Drake had been on *Degrassi*.

"Yeah, well, everyone loves her. Now I'm the asshole who publicly broke Kylie Cameron's heart."

Hunter squinted at the phone again. If the Kinsey scale was a reliable measure—as a medical doctor, he had his doubts—Hunter was a solid six. Unambiguously gay. And usually he was ruthlessly adept at not developing crushes on straight guys. (Gay guys who pretended to be straight in certain circumstances were another question. Unfortunately.) So the image of Jesse Jamison kissing Ms. Anonymous should have had no effect on him. He should have been immune.

But damn, there was something about that picture. The way Jesse was crowding his not-girlfriend up against the wall. The way he was framing her face with his hands. That was why only her hair was visible—Jesse's hands were clamped possessively on her face.

And if Jesse had this much to lose by being spotted, the fact that this kiss had gone down in public must have meant they'd both been pretty carried away. Hunter shifted in his seat.

"What's her name?" He handed the phone back with an odd reluctance.

"My girlfriend? You mean her real name? It's Kylie—she never used a stage name. And I should probably start calling her my *ex*-girlfriend. 'Cause she is not going to stand for this shit."

"No." Hunter gestured to the phone. "What's the other woman's name?"

Jesse paused before answering. "It doesn't really matter."

"You don't know it!" Damn, this guy *was* a rock star, or at least well on his way to becoming one. Hunter cracked up; he couldn't help it. Jesse certainly looked the part. Choppy dark, messy hair hung around his face. His forearms—he wore a ratty flannel shirt with the sleeves rolled up—were covered with tattoos. He had that kind of sexy-sleazy look.

That was not a look Hunter went for.

Historically.

He liked a more polished look.

Usually.

"Haven't you ever made out with someone whose name you didn't catch?" Jesse asked.

"Not for a really long time." Not since before he'd met Julian. And even before Julian, Hunter had been a serial monogamist. He could count on one hand the number of casual hookups in his past.

Maybe that was what the move to Toronto had been missing so far—some casual sex to break him out of his slump. The prospect was kind of terrifying.

"Well, you should try it," Jesse declared. "Quickest way to get over your loser ex."

"Why do you assume my ex was the loser? Maybe I was the loser."

"Nah."

Hunter wanted to ask how Jesse could possibly know this, but he didn't want to make it seem like he was fishing for compliments.

Jesse's phone buzzed. He picked it up again. "And there it is."

"What?"

Jessie scrolled for a moment, then said, "The breakup text." He sighed resignedly.

"Really?" Hunter was taken aback by the idea of breaking up with someone via text, but he supposed that was part of the jet-set, rock star life his seatmate lived. "Jesus, I'm sorry."

Jesse shrugged. "It's okay. Saves me having to do it. The writing was already on the wall."

"The writing on the wall being something *other than* you making out with someone else against the wall? It seems like your whole problem here is the wall."

All he got in response was a chuckle.

Clearly, Jesse was not the type to invest his heart and soul and the better part of a decade into a relationship.

Hunter should learn from Jesse.

He was downloading Grindr as soon as he got home.

"The more important question is whether my *manager* is going to dump me over this."

"You're more concerned about getting dumped by your manager than your girlfriend?" Hunter asked, though he wasn't sure why—the answer was clear.

"I have a bit of a work-life balance problem?" Jesse shrugged. "And also a manager who basically has me on probation."

"Wow." Who *was* this guy? Hunter had never seen anyone so…unapologetic.

"What are you drinking?" Jesse asked.

"What?" Oh, the service cart was making its way down the aisle.

"I'm guessing whiskey isn't your preferred poison."

When Hunter didn't answer right away, Jesse dropped his magazines into the seat pocket in front of him and said, "Fuck career-ruining photographs." Then he did the same with his phone, holding it between one finger and a thumb like it was contaminated. "Fuck dying kids. Fuck *everyone*. We're single and free. We should toast that shit."

* * *

Four hours later, as the conductor announced they were ten minutes from Union Station, Jesse was feeling good.

Eight mini-bottles of red wine could have that effect on a guy.

"We should hide the evidence," Hunter said, slurring a bit

and then laughing. He'd only had four mini-bottles. The handsome doctor *was* a bit of a lightweight.

It was adorable.

Jesse had procured most of the aforementioned mini-bottles by sweet-talking a young woman porter after the older man assigned to their car responded to Jesse's request for bottle number four by looking down his nose and saying, "There's only an hour left on your journey, sir."

Hunter reached toward the small garbage bag the train provided, his bottles in hand.

"Hey, no need to 'hide the evidence.'" Jesse grabbed Hunter's arm near the elbow to halt his tidying instinct. Maybe Jesse was an entitled rock star asshole, but he planned to leave a pile of tiny bottles on the seat for the snotty porter to deal with.

Hunter was wearing one of those shirts that looked like flannel, but were actually made of some kind of unbelievably soft mystery material. It was hard to take his hand away. It was hard to do anything but let his hand slide down a forearm that was softer than...all the soft things. A cat? A cloud? A—

—hand.

He'd reached the bare skin of the back of Hunter's hand, and the change in texture was so jarring, he snatched his own hand away as if he'd touched a hot stove.

"No need to hide the evidence, because there was no crime," he said firmly. "These baby boozes were procured with cold, hard cash."

"Cold hard cash and a boatload of charm," Hunter said, and Jesse didn't have an argument for that one. "What about public drunkenness?" Hunter went on. "Isn't that a crime?"

"You might have me there."

Except not. He wasn't nearly drunk enough to plug back

into reality. He fished for his phone, dread in his gut. He knew what he would find. Outraged tweets from the public that he had dared to cheat on their beloved Kylie. Incredulous texts from the guys. Anger from his manager, who had read him the riot act about his out-of-control behavior only a month ago.

And there it was.

His second breakup text of the day.

He'd been fired by his manager. Cut loose by the woman who had plucked the band out of the club scene and deftly shepherded them to the next level—they were now routinely selling out midsize venues, and she'd been talking about a major-label deal when they were done with their current indie contract.

It stung like hell. *Way* more than Kylie.

He glanced at Dr. Wyatt the Baby Silver Fox, who was shrugging into his coat.

Since they were approaching the station, Jesse stood and moved into the aisle.

"Well, thanks for the…boozy chat." Hunter stood too, but he lost his footing, and Jesse had to grab him to steady him.

"Whoa," Jesse said, liking the feel of the scratchy wool of Hunter's coat under his fingers. Hunter, with his fuzzy coat and his cottony soft shirt, had Jesse on tactile overload. "Maybe there was too much booze in that chat."

"No." Hunter flashed an impish, satisfied smile. The kind of smile Jesse could imagine coming up in…other contexts. "That was the *perfect balance* of booze and conversation. You made me forget all about my dead dog and my broken heart."

Broken heart. Hunter had been vague about his breakup earlier. It was hard to imagine someone as confident, as obviously accomplished, as *solid* as Hunter getting his heart broken.

It was hard to imagine any man giving him up.

Any man who was in the stage of life and career that promoted being settled and monogamous, that was.

And out.

Which was not Jesse. Not even close.

Which was why he couldn't explain why the next thing he did was dig around in his bag until he found a receipt and a pen, scrawled his email and phone number on it, and said, "Keep in touch."

* * *

"Give me one reason I should sign a punk like you?"

Jesse blinked. He was hungover, and his mind was slow. He had gone home last night after that surreal train ride and graduated from mini-bottles of booze to a full-size one. And, in a state of drunken overconfidence-mixed-with-defiance, he'd emailed Matty Alvarado, Canada's most famous artist manager. The guy oversaw a handful of successful musical exports, youngish pop stars mostly, who'd made it big south of the border and beyond. He was known as a rainmaker.

There was no way he'd take on a medium-time rock-and-roll band like Jesse and the Joyride.

Or so Jesse had thought.

But here he was twenty-four hours later, having been summoned to the dude's palatial office, which was decorated with a weird mixture of Catholic paraphernalia and photos of Matty with some of the world's most popular acts.

"You have quite the reputation, you know," Matty went on when Jesse didn't answer fast enough. "The Canadian music scene is small. People talk."

"We've been steadily building momentum for the last

couple years." Jesse started in on the speech he'd been rehearsing in his head on the way over. "We've been playing midsize venues. I'm getting better and better as a songwriter. We have one more record left on our contract. After that, a major-label deal is within reach—I know it."

Matty waved a hand dismissively, like all of Jesse's painstaking, incremental work was nothing more than a bit of lint to be brushed off. "There's no shortage of acts in your position. Wannabe rock stars with big dreams are a dime a dozen, so you—"

"We're good," Jesse said, daring to interrupt the famed tastemaker, because why not? This wasn't going well, and he had nothing to lose. "No, we're fucking *great*."

Matty sighed. Drummed his fingers on his huge lacquered desk. "You are," he finally said, as if it pained him to admit it. "But you're also a fucking mess. Look at you—hungover, splashed all over the tabloids every couple of months with some drama or other. That's what I expect from the teenagers I sign, Jesse, not from grown men. What I do is brand people. I *make* them. I can make something from nothing, no problem. But I don't know that I can make something from…a big pile of shit."

Jesse winced.

"Coming back from cheating on Kylie Cameron might be impossible," Matty said.

Might be.

Those two words surged through Jesse. They were a thin edge of crowbar he could use to pry open this door.

Jesse had spent his entire life striving to get where he was. He'd had to beg his parents for piano lessons, for second-hand guitars. Later, when he'd been a bit older, he would have moved into the band room in his high school if his teacher had let him. It had literally been his happy place. Some days, it had felt like his *only* place.

Music was his life. It had been from the start.

And, just as importantly, it was his *living*. He was making a living as a musician. Or he had been, anyway.

All he wanted—the dream he'd had since he'd been old enough to dream—was to be on the cover of *Rolling Stone*.

And he could get there. All the ingredients were in place.

The only thing standing in his way was him.

That's what Matty was saying, and suddenly, Jesse *got* it.

"The way I see it," he started slowly, thinking through his argument with a mind suddenly cleared of cobwebs, "is that the *GossipTO* article was a blessing in disguise."

Matty raised an eyebrow. "That's the first interesting thing you've said since you got here."

"Kylie told me something once. She said that everyone performs who they are to some degree. Despite having gotten her start on a TV show, she had no aspirations to cross back over into acting, but she said she was an actor all the same. 'We all are,' she said. 'All of us whose livelihoods depend on being in the public eye. We perform who we are, consciously or no. The trick to success is to understand this and to learn to exploit it. Learn how to control the performance. Be in control of your own narrative.'"

He had dismissed her approach as too Machiavellian, but he saw now that she'd been right.

"Smart woman." Matty made a "go on" gesture.

"The way I see it, I have two choices. I can live like a rock star—partying, coming in late to recording sessions because I'm hungover, slutting around with anything that moves."

Which was exactly what he'd been doing. He'd been too

busy with his degenerate life lately to prioritize what mattered: the music.

"Or…" he continued, trying to formulate his thoughts into a coherent argument. "I can *act* like a rock star."

"What does that mean?"

"I don't know. You tell me. You sign me, and I'll do whatever you tell me to do. But only on the surface. Underneath that, I'm keeping my head down. Cutting way, way back on the booze so I'm clearheaded enough to make kick-ass music and smart business decisions. Keeping my dick in my pants."

Matty was silent a long time, then he said, "Do we need to send you to rehab?"

We. He'd said, *We.* Adrenaline started frothing in Jesse's veins.

"No. Let me give it a shot, and if it doesn't work, I'll go without argument." He was pretty sure now that he'd had his come-to-Jesus moment—maybe all that Catholic stuff on Matty's walls had put the whammy on him—making the necessary lifestyle changes was going to be easy.

"Drugs?"

"Not really. The odd joint to relax after the show if someone offers, but I'm not buying the stuff. And I'll drop that too, if you want."

"No one wants their rock stars to be saints," said Matty. "It's a fine line."

"I get that," said Jesse. That was kind of what he'd been trying to articulate with the whole *live like a rock star versus act like a rock star* thing.

"Fuck me, but I think you do," said Matty. "The question is, are you all talk?"

Jesse smiled, feeling some of his old swagger returning. "There's only one way to find out."

"This is how it's going to work," Matty said. "You and I sign a contract for six months. Consider it a probationary period. A tryout. You know that whole three strikes, you're out thing?"

Jesse nodded and tried not to grin too overtly.

"With you and me, it's one strike. You do the music. I do everything else. You do exactly what I say. I tell you you're going on Howard Stern, you're going on Howard Stern. I say you're going on the Mickey Mouse Club, you're going on the Mickey Mouse Club. I get you a girlfriend, you've got a girl-friend. I tell you to break up with her, you break up with her. I say you're playing a show at the North fucking Pole, you're out shopping for snowsuits. After six months, we regroup. If we both want to continue—and if you've behaved yourself—we sign for real. Got it?"

"Yes." Jesse refrained from babbling about how grateful he was. Matty didn't seem like the kind of guy who appreciated empty words, and Jesse respected that.

"Is there anything else I need to know about? Any other scandals brewing? If I don't know about it, I can't fix it."

Jesse hesitated. As much as he hated to do it, it was prob-ably wise to lay all his cards on the table.

"What?"

"That...person in the photo from *GossipTO*..."

"She going to talk to the press?" Matty did the dismissive waving thing again. "That's no problem. We can spin that to our advantage."

"I don't think so. It's more that she...wasn't a she."

Matty blinked rapidly.

"But I don't think he actually knew who I was," Jesse continued quickly. "We didn't really talk, and he didn't say anything about recognizing me. I met him at—"

"What are you saying, Jesse? You're gay? Because that is not going to work with the brand I'm envisioning for you."

"Not gay. Bisexual. And not even that much." It was true. Jesse thought of himself as mostly straight but...open to other possibilities. But he figured Matty probably didn't care about shades of gray here.

Matty got up and walked around to the front of his desk. Jesse stood, thinking he was being dismissed. *Fuck.* That picture really *had* ruined his life. He'd had the biggest agent in all of Canada *almost* locked down.

"Sit." Matty leaned back against the front of his desk, like he was a school principal.

Jesse sat.

"I don't want to hear another word about this. From this point onward, you are not...*bisexual*." Matty spat the word like it was a curse. "You are Jesse Jamison, the bad-boy rock star next door. What does that mean? You're a fucking rock star. As I said, no one wants you to be a saint. You're brilliant and prickly and you live large. Or rather, you give the appearance of living large. You do what you need to do to keep yourself clean enough that your head is in the game, but you are not to speak publicly about having a problem with booze or any of that. Jesse Jamison the recovering alcoholic is not what we're going for here. When you appear at high-profile events, you have a fucking craft beer in your hand. You're single now, and we're going to use that. You are going to date casually. You are going to break a heart or two. All that's the rock star part. But you have a soft side. You're a little vulnerable. A sixteen-year-old girl can imagine reforming you. She can imagine you taking her to the fucking prom. Hell, I might make you actually do that. That's the boy-next-door side."

Jesse could see where Matty was going with this. It made

sense. Matty's "brand," as much as Jesse hated that word, picked up on Jesse's natural tendencies and...magnified them.

Well, *some* of his natural tendencies.

"But one thing I need to be absolutely clear about is that both the rock star and the boy next door are straight. Those hearts you're breaking are *female* hearts. Those teenagers fantasizing about you are *female* teenagers. If you don't agree one hundred percent with this right now, we're done."

Something pinged inside Jesse's chest, like a pebble being dropped into an empty box. And for some stupid reason, he thought of Dr. Hunter Wyatt, the heartbroken pediatrician.

Then he thought of the cover of *Rolling Stone*. He thought of what he'd been striving for his whole goddamn life.

He stuck his hand out. "It's a deal."

www.ingramcontent.com/pod-product-compliance
Lightning Source LLC
Chambersburg PA
CBHW052041240626
47153CB00006B/2177